PROCESSION OF SHADOWS

OTHER WORKS BY JULIÁN RÍOS IN ENGLISH TRANSLATION

Larva: Midsummer Night's Babel
Poundemonium
Kitaj: Pictures and Conversations
Loves That Bind
Monstruary
The House of Ulysses

PROCESSION OF SHADOWS
(THE NOVEL OF TAMOGA)

JULIÁN RÍOS
Translated by Nick Caistor

With a Foreword by the Author

DALKEY ARCHIVE PRESS
CHAMPAIGN AND LONDON

Originally published in Spanish as *Cortejo de sombras* by Círculo de Lectores,
S. A. (Sociedad Unipersonal)/Galaxia Gutenberg, 2007
Copyright © 2007 by Julián Ríos
Translation copyright © 2011 by Nick Caistor
First edition, 2011
All rights reserved

Library of Congress Cataloging-in-Publication Data

Ríos, Julián.
[Cortejo de sombras. English]
Procession of shadows / Julian Rios ; translated by Nick Caistor. -- 1st ed.
    p. cm.
Originally published in Spanish as Cortejo de sombras in 2007.
ISBN 978-1-56478-634-0 (pbk. : acid-free paper)
I. Caistor, Nick. II. Title.
PQ6668.I576C6713 2011
863'.64--dc22
                              2011002829

Partially funded by the University of Illinois at Urbana-Champaign, as well as by grants
from the National Endowment for the Arts, a federal agency, and the Illinois Arts Council,
a state agency

This work has been published with a subsidy from the Directorate General of Books,
Archives and Libraries of the Spanish Ministry of Culture

www.dalkeyarchive.com

Cover: design and composition by Danielle Dutton, illustration by Nicholas Motte
Printed on permanent/durable acid-free paper and bound in the United States of America

CONTENTS

FOREWORD:

TAMOGA REVISITED

I wrote *Procession of Shadows* between 1966 and 1968 in Madrid (at the time I was trying to relive and recreate without resorting to regionalisms my very own Galicia, the land of marvels of my childhood and adolescence, with its occasionally ominous shadows from the past, into which was mixed, in a nostalgic, phantomlike way, the country of leaving-never-to-return that so many emigrants have known). When I went to live in London in 1969, I took the manuscript with me, intending to add a couple of chapters I had already roughed out. In the end I decided to leave the book as it was, and only revised and corrected the chapter entitled "Palonzo." Although the nine chapters can stand on their own as short stories, I always thought of them as forming part of a choral novel about an imaginary town and space, with characters revealing the events of their lives and the lives of others in a way that was to a greater or lesser extent interrelated.

Some of these stories won prizes—for example "Second Person" won the Gabriel Miró prize in 1969, and "The River Without Banks" the Hucha de Plata for short stories in 1970, but I never felt inclined to send the novel to a publisher. I assumed the censors wouldn't allow chapters such as "Hunting in July" to be published, but there were other reasons to postpone publication of the book. The main one was that, a year after I moved to London, I embarked on the narrative project that became *Larva*, which turned out to be as broad as it was long, because it involved widening out the Spanish language and removing its obsession with castles in Spain so that it could reflect the crossbreeding and polyglot cosmopolitanism of the great capital city as a microcosm of the entire world. I therefore decided it was better for *Procession of Shadows* to remain in the shadows and not see the light of day in the oppressive country I was leaving behind, while the carnival Trickster of my new novel went on chasing women and the shadows of the night on the banks of the Thames. In the free life of London, where I was caught up in the games of love and language and masks of *Larva*, I left *Procession of Shadows* behind, or perhaps felt I no longer really understood the plain Spanish of the rainy plains.

Early one January morning in 1970, in a snowy London, after having dinner with friends in Golders Green in the northwest of the city, I met a taxi driver who turned out to be from Tamoga, or a very similar town close by. He had come to England aged seven or eight, and after twenty-five years had almost completely forgotten his mother tongue. He tried to speak odd sentences in Spanish that I helped him to complete or pronounce more clearly. After we had reached my destination, further south in Queen's Park, we sat a good hour practicing the basic Spanish of his surprise bout of homesickness, while the white flakes that had already covered the park opposite enveloped his cab. With each phrase painfully pulled from his brain came a shred of memory. Attached to the freshly rediscovered language was his brief childhood in Tamoga. That London taxi driver, a few years older than me, was trying to reclaim his lost language and past. I on the other hand had come to London to forget them, to escape from a suffocating atmosphere and country. It's with good reason that the sign on the Tamoga station platform, with its two missing letters, spells out *A[h]oga* (Drowning). With hindsight, which offers the best perspective, I can see that I was trying to get away from a Spain that smelled to me of mothballs, if not downright fishy, a country which doubtless hurt me less than Unamuno, whose famous pronouncement is farcically paraphrased and faithfully translated by the narrator of Larva when he exclaims: "Spain pains me!" It seemed to me then that to subvert language was the best aspirin to fight the headache of being isolated beyond the Pyrenees barrier.

The years and books went by, as well as other cities I've lived in, and the typescript of *Procession of Shadows* remained at the bottom of a trunk waiting for me to take the trouble to blow the dust off it and take another look. With time, I could not help but feel a certain remorse whenever I recalled it. For example, in 1991, when I was living in Berlin, I considered offering an excerpt for a feature that a German magazine was preparing on me, but found I did not have the manuscript with me. A few years later, during an over-dinner conversation in New York with one of my North American editors when we were talking about the Franco days in Spain, I brought up the subject of my unpublished book, which seemed like a youthful sin forever consigned to purgatory. Then, a year and a half ago, when I was talking to my French editors in Paris, *Procession* emerged from the shadows to appear in our conversation and aroused an interest I was not sure I shared at the time.

A few months passed after that other dinner-table conversation in Paris, and I found that in the novel I'm writing, among the memories of one of the characters—someone as uprooted as the taxi driver in London—some distant images of Tamoga appeared. I told myself I needed to pay Tamoga another visit. So, for the first time since 1970, and with some trepidation, I sat down to read *Procession of Shadows*. I did not feel any paternal tenderness or nostalgia toward it, but neither was I overwhelmed by any expiatory pseudomasochistic impulse or serious objections. I am other: another author. Who of course bears the marks of the twists, turns, and upturns of his time. Or as Milalias, the protagonist of *Larva* might say, divinely: *Yo soy el que es hoy* (I am he who is today) . . . In reality, after so many years, *Procession of Shadows* left me no option but to become its reader, and there was, therefore, nothing for me to add or subtract. So I am pleased the book has not become *Confusion of Shadows*, a mixture of the original text and new, extemporaneous additions and corrections: the author I was then combined with the one I am now.

I particularly like the procession of form and style in *Procession of Shadows*, two things I have always tried to give equal weight in my writing. I also like the part the characters play in the narration, another of my loves that bind: climbing into another person's skin.

As I finish writing these lines, I can see out my window a cargo boat sailing down the Seine opposite Île de Saint-Martin, passing the village of Vétheuil, and disappearing around another bend in the river near the house where Monet lived. I already know the course of the Seine by heart, so I can anticipate that, later on, near the city of Rouen, it will pass by Flaubert's cottage in Croisset, then reach the estuary, head out to sea, and perhaps after many hours and waves it will be off the coast of Tamoga, which has often, also, been the coast of death.

J.R.

PROCESSION OF SHADOWS

I.

MORTES'S STORY

It was toward the end of September, when the drowsiness of autumn was beginning to make itself felt; the hours went by more slowly and time itself seemed to stagnate like the forlorn waters of the salt marshes around Tamoga.

"A traveling salesman," said or thought absentmindedly all the bored men gathered in the station with nothing better to do as dusk fell when they saw first the enormous suitcase and then the short man comically veering from side to side in his efforts to drag it along the platform. "A dung beetle," someone in the group joked, trying to breathe new life into their flagging conversation. They stared at the stranger for a few moments longer, but nobody could be bothered to add another comment. They watched the train disappear into the endless rain, feeling a twinge of disappointment, a nostalgia for times past.

That man, the stranger, perhaps himself never even knew why he had chosen this town. Or perhaps it was not he who had chosen it, but chance, fate, his lucky or unlucky star, one inevitability leading to another.

We learned afterward that he had agreed to meet a woman in the town, and that she—still young, almost beautiful, with the look of someone recently widowed—was his sister-in-law. We learned from Inspector Cardona the story of his flight, their crazy love affair. We also learned (she, the sister-in-law, allowed herself to be interrogated at length by the inspector; sad but serene, proud of her love, docile and disbelieving in the end, past caring about anything or anyone) that his name was Mortes and that he was a traveling salesman, that he was soon to be fifty, had a wife and five children, and a blameless past. Everything very ordinary and inoffensive, depressing. And yet it seemed that he, Mortes—the least mysterious man in the world—had come to our town to play out an apparently absurd little farce.

For us, for our curiosity, it all began one Tuesday in September at the start of autumn, the day he arrived. From the window of his second-class compartment, Mortes would have gazed out at the rain-swept platform, the faded sign with the letters *T* and *M* almost completely worn away, so that it read A OGA. He would have been greeted by a jumble of clouds and roofs. Seeing this, he must have thought the town was gloomy enough for what he had in mind. It's also likely that what persuaded him to get off the train at the last moment was weariness, boredom, the conviction that he had never been in this town before; the certainty that he would not be recognized, that he had never dragged his huge leather trunk through the streets of Tamoga or put on his professional smile in any of its stores or businesses. He must also have known and felt relieved that he had never leaned on any counter chatting to the inevitable old maid about ribbons and buttons with the restrained passion, the secretive air, of someone making an indecent proposal. It's also likely he was attracted by the town's location and the fact it was so close to the border (we came to suspect this later on, when the woman appeared), not to mention that from the start he thought he could rely on our stupidity and collective curiosity, our lack of foresight—although none of these suppositions help explain the end of this story, if it can be said to have an end. It might also simply have been that he was crazy or scared. Or possibly he got caught up in his own game, the impossible lie he wanted to believe.

As I said, he, Mortes, arrived in Tamoga at the start of autumn on a sad, rainy day. Despite the fact that he was only among us for a few hours, he is still remembered with great relish, especially because of how his story ended; many people swear not only to have seen him, but to have talked with him. He had the gift of metamorphosis, apparently, because each one of us remembers him differently—although it's possible that all of our impressions were equally correct: happy, timid, forlorn, a joker, sneering, respectful, cynical, dull, likeable: he is all those things in our accounts of him. In the end we're left with fascination, and the impossibility of telling his story, because in this case the words are more concrete than the facts, and a story is really only worth telling when words can't exhaust its meaning. We're also free to imagine and attribute multiple, contradictory, and obscure objectives to that rather short, rather skinny, rather ungainly stranger who chose Tamoga as the stage for his performance. Now Mortes is nothing more than words and a vague image already beginning to fade in our memory: a broad face with ill-defined features, dun colored, as if made out of mud. His eyes were red-rimmed and his mouth a slash; his voice a nasal drawl that sometimes turned into a deep gurgling like the sound of water running through pipes. An unremarkable man who wore (not elegantly, but not shabbily either) a crumpled brown suit and an oversized trench coat. That is how we see Mortes in our memory, and that is how Don Elío, the stationmaster, must have seen him that first afternoon.

"You get used to all kinds, especially at my age and this being a frontier station," old Don Elío will have said. "But there must've been something wrong with that one—he wasn't quite right in the head. Look: he was on the quarter-past-seven train, which that day was almost on time. It always stops here for five minutes, that's long enough. I rang the bell for it to depart and right across from me saw the man suddenly leap up from his seat and rush into the corridor with his trunk. He got off just as the train was pulling out. Because he was just absentminded, maybe? Well, listen: thirty seconds before, he had been staring calmly out of his compartment window. He looked at the people on the platform, at me, at the station, smoking as calmly as though he was going somewhere else, as if he wasn't at all concerned that this station was Tamoga, though the big sign was there right in front of his nose. He heard the bell as if it was a call to Mass and then, at the very last moment, he was in a rush, jumping off the moving train with his trunk and everything. He almost killed himself. You should have seen him: standing there on the platform as if he had fallen from heaven, arms out wide like a scarecrow."

In any event, he wasn't a statue there for too long. He headed for the main exit and walked out into the rain and blustery wind of Tamoga. The taxi drivers sitting bored in their cabs outside the station watched him cross the square without any hope of a fare. He waved the porters away too, and dragged his trunk over to the coach parked under the plane trees. He sat with the other few passengers in the ramshackle bus, staring blankly out at the rain and the square, the dripping trees, and the showy sign by the side of the main road proclaiming in red letters: WELCOME TO TAMOGA, until One-Armed Gómez, the conductor, appeared in front of him. According to Gómez, the stranger looked like he was convalescing or completely exhausted, as if he had been in a hospital or was returning from a long trip. The stranger dried his face with a handkerchief and patted his shoulders to shake off the raindrops. He asked how much a ticket was, and how far it was to town. He seemed relieved at the answers, as though he was in a hurry and the three kilometers were one less thing to worry about. He sat examining his ticket, as if the small pink piece of paper announcing *Bus Service Tamoga/Station or Vice-Versa* was an object of great interest. After a while, he raised his head:

"Perhaps you can help me . . . Do you happen to know of a hotel without too many bedbugs or fleas?" he asked the conductor with a smile.

"I mentioned the London Hotel," Gómez said. "I don't know why, but I took a liking to him. Perhaps because he was different from the passengers I usually get. He put the coins in my left hand, and made no fuss when he saw my stump. He seemed to find it quite natural that a conductor might have an arm or a leg missing, so long as he doesn't let anyone get away without paying. After that he said thanks, pressed his face to the window, and stared out at the marshes the whole time until we got into town."

He took a room at the London, wrote his name and all his details in the hotel register, putting up the whole time with Doña Milagros's rude stare. As usual, she was sitting bolt upright on her wheelchair throne behind the counter, knitting. (In our sentimental way, some of us suspected that Doña Milagros opened the hotel not simply to show everyone in Tamoga how resilient and capable she was—that she was in no way an invalid and would never accept pity from anyone—but also in the secret hope that one day her husband would make a nostalgic leap back to Tamoga. He had abandoned her in the middle of their honeymoon when she had her accident; terrified at the thought of all that this implied—with no money or job, and unable to bear his wife's temper a day longer, in a moment of lucid panic he must have glimpsed the inferno awaiting him. In those days they lived close to the Portuguese quarter, in a house belonging to one of Doña Milagros's uncles. An old bachelor, he was miserly and eccentric. He had sworn to leave everything to his niece if she looked after him in his last illness (like all old people, in his desire to go on living he must have promised himself a slow and difficult death), even though he steadfastly refused to give her a penny before then. Those were hard years. One morning like any other, her husband said goodbye in his usual unenthusiastic way, with his habitual forced smile: "I'm going down to the port. An English boat has arrived." That was the last time Doña Milagros ever heard his voice. A short while later, the old man died, as if he had only been waiting for his niece's husband to abscond to close his eyes in peace. With the inheritance money, Doña Milagros decided to open a hotel, rejecting the advice of those who told her she should live off her income. Ever since, she has sat at all hours in the hotel lobby, keeping a curious and watchful eye on everything, kept upright in her wheelchair by hope and an ancient premonition—if her husband should come back one day, he might come to stay in the London, foolishly attracted as many visitors were by the hotel's cosmopolitan name, and unaware that the mummy-newlywed was lying in wait for him, knitting and unraveling her revenge— shamelessly studying everyone who came to stay, trying to compare their faces with the features already fading in the old images stored in her memory, or, perhaps, simply trying to assess how capable they are of paying their bill.)

So Mortes put up with Doña Milagros's piercing stare, asked for a single room with a bathroom, and said he had no idea how long he would be staying in Tamoga. "One day, two, or maybe a week. It depends on how things go," he said as he filled in the form. "Or perhaps I'll spend the rest of my life here," he added, winking at the old woman, trying to make a joke, which she didn't find funny.

After this comes the detailed report from Alcides, one of Doña Milagros's countless godsons. Enveloped in his customary black suit, funereal and anxious to please as ever, and with his fussy homosexual gestures and oozing the sickly sweet rhetoric of a former seminarian, his head shining, perfumed, and pomaded, Alcides appeared in the lobby to take Mortes's suitcase, after a half-hearted struggle, then lead the stranger to his room on the first floor.

"The suitcase was heavy, like it was full of books or lead, or had a dead body in it," Alcides said in his exaggerated way.

"That'll do; you can leave it on the bed," Mortes told him.

He didn't seem disappointed by the small, dark room situated at the rear of the hotel.

He pushed back the faded lace curtain and peered out. From this height he could see the ground covered in puddles and piles of trash, and opposite, the warehouses and shacks where the Portuguese lived. Further off were the bare, windswept hillsides, and the still, gray water lapping the horizon.

He walked around the room several times, carefully stuck his hand in the tear in the wallpaper, expecting to find a nest of bedbugs or something worse. Opening the wardrobe, he poked his head inside and with the back of his hand raised a sad arpeggio from the row of metal hangers. He continued his painstaking inspection: he went into the bathroom, pulled the lavatory chain, took a step back when he heard the water gushing ominously. He switched on the light, studied himself in the mirror for a few seconds, and rubbed his hands across his cheeks as if he needed to confirm he had several days' growth of beard. Finally, he turned on both taps in the washbasin.

"There's no hot water," he said, with the look of someone who's just discovered he's been swindled.

"It only comes on in the mornings," sighed Alcides, weary of repeating the same phrase for the past eight years.

Mortes returned to the bedroom and saw with satisfaction that it contained two wicker armchairs, a portable lamp on the bedside table, a big china ashtray, and a bottle of water covered with a glass. Perhaps he wanted to seem demanding, as though he was going to spend several days in Tamoga and wanted to choose someplace comfortable.

"Haberdashery or fabrics?" asked Alcides, eager to earn his tip.

Alarmed at the cigarette burn on the bedspread and the patch of damp on the wall that looked like an enormous crab about to plummet onto the pillow, Mortes took a few moments to respond.

"A bit of everything," was his eventual unenthusiastic answer, aimed at the window or no one.

"I can give you information about the stores here," Alcides suggested, anxious to get to the point.

"He didn't seem interested," Alcides was to complain afterwards. "He pushed the crumpled edge of the rug straight, and turned toward me with an upset, almost disgusted gesture, as if I was trying to involve him in some dirty business."

"'Listen,' I said to him confidentially. 'Just listen. There are stores in this town that look very grand, look wonderful from the outside, and yet they've had the same stuff on show in their windows for half a century. I'm not exaggerating. How do they manage to survive? Don't ask: nobody knows. We have shops in the center of town (yes, you'll see them right outside) with windows as big as this, and signs that read Sons of So and So, Inheritors of What's His Name, House Founded in 1860, Latest Fashions from Paris, all very fancy. But if you go in, all you see is dust, fly droppings, and goods from the year zero, all of them moth-eaten or rotting away. They sell a few bits and pieces when the market is going and the country people from Páramos and Santa Cruz come into town, along with the fishermen from Providencia and Puerto Angra. But that's about all. Believe me: they're dead as doornails. You're wasting your time if you try to sell them anything novel or fashionable.'

"At this point I always pause for effect, with the salesmen passing through, before suggesting the names of shopkeepers who *do* have money and are interested in new products. Despite all my best efforts, this had no effect on him. He only grimaced, as though to say: well, what can you do . . .

"'Thanks,' he said, as if making excuses for himself. 'Thanks, but I don't need a guide . . . I like to survey the field of battle first, to work out for myself where I might bomb or make a killing, if you follow me?'

"What can you do with someone like that? By then I wasn't worried about my tip; it was a matter of pride, of being annoyed by his condescension. That's when I started to become suspicious. I've met more than enough salesmen, and all of them are curious, especially when they arrive in a town for the first time and don't know a soul. Show me a single one who isn't curious. Well, he immediately tried to make amends; he took a crumpled twenty-five peseta note out of his pocket, smoothed it, and gave it to me with a smile.

"'We'll see in the morning,' he said, dismissing me.

"I was already out in the hall when I heard his nasal, world-weary voice once more:

"'What's there to do in a place like this in the evening or at night?' he asked, clearing his throat and jigging about comically.

"Aha! I thought. So he was one of those who like to put a brave face on things. A proper night owl, I'm sure.

"'This is a boring town,' I said without bitterness, but not wanting to lie. 'Though we do have three movie theaters. On Tuesdays only the Moderno is open. Today they're showing a Spanish film: *The Invincible Amada* or something like that, I can't remember exactly. We have too many bars and inns. At the weekends there are two dance halls. And then there's the Terranova. It's open every night until dawn.'

"By now he was listening closely, trying to imagine from what I was saying how sad a coastal town can be after the summer season. I went on listing the possibilities for amusement in Tamoga, thinking I was getting my revenge and that he was going to feel the depressing weight of the hours here, how long a night can be in this purgatory.

" 'There used to be several houses where you could have fun down by the river,' I recalled, overcome by a sense of nostalgia. I remembered Materno the eunuch when he came with his five eternal virgins, and the love lottery in the ruins of the old salted-fish factory. Those were the good times, when the mineral-loading bay was functioning. 'But all that's gone now,' I told him, 'and our only house of ill repute is the Terranova. You can listen to music there, dance, have a drink or two, and if you're not too fussy, find some female company. You'll at least always have the comfort of seeing other faces as bored as your own—and, if you're lucky, you might make it back to the hotel with the memory of some not-too-horrible woman. Although I couldn't guarantee that, I must say.' "

Later on, when everything was apparently over and done with, Inspector Cardona, who was a stickler for routine and always wanted to discover a logical sequence of events in matters that quite possibly had none, tried to reconstruct the stranger's movements so that there would be no gaps in our knowledge of the short span of time that Mortes spent among us.

He, Mortes, must have spent a couple of hours stretched out on the bed in his room (the imprint of his body on the bedspread was still there the next morning as proof that he had not spent the night in the London, but that, likewise, he wasn't a ghost, and had really existed in Tamoga for a few hours at least), going over his regrets and his plans, getting drunk on dreams, cradling his fear as he listened to the sound of the rain on the windowpanes, perhaps thinking as he lay facing the wall: "I'm here in a town surrounded by the sea and I have no idea what I'm going to do."

By the time he left the room he had probably already made up his mind, had understood (without rancor or regret) that he still had to perform the final act, had to show himself to his public, gather his strength so as not to have to be prompted, to take a bow as the curtain fell.

From the hotel Mortes must have gone directly to Prado's restaurant on Avenida Portugal. Perhaps he was tempted by the yellow lettering that falsely claimed: *Our Specialty: All Kinds of Seafood*. Perhaps he was hungry, or thought this was a reasonable time to have dinner and so pretend to be hungry. "He ordered a salad, sirloin with fried potatoes, fruit, and half a bottle of red," Prado reported *meticulously*. "He ate in a hurry, gobbling it down. Between each mouthful he stared at the pinup girl with the big backside on the calendar opposite him. He paid without leaving a tip, and asked where he could find a pharmacy open at that time of night."

He was seen in the town hall square, at the far end of town. He asked the night watchman which drugstore might still have a pharmacist on duty, and let himself be led to the street corner and then came to a halt beneath a metal sign reading "Rocha Pharmacy." Before going in, he peered at both the windows and at the lighted interior.

Severino the pharmacy assistant attended him. "He asked me for some sleeping pills," Severino said, "but first he wandered around the shelves, as if he was interested in all the pots with their gold lettering, or hadn't yet decided what he was after. Then he came and stood with his hands on the glass counter, his head tilted to one side as though he was still undecided or was trying to remember something. He looked bored and in need of conversation. He asked for some pills that would make him sleep properly: like a dead man, he added, with a wry grin. I don't think he often took sleeping tablets, because otherwise he would have asked for a particular brand. He offered me a cigarette and started to complain about the climate here. He said that by all rights the inhabitants of this region ought to have evolved gills by now, then asked how many pharmacies there were in town, and if people here were naïve or trusting enough to believe in medicines and to see a doctor when they were dying. Jokingly, he asked me with that sly grin he had—twisting his lip—if in the provinces and in such a wet place as this there was much call for rubber goods, condoms and the like."

Now it was time for the love song. Either before or after visiting the pharmacy, Mortes went to the telephone exchange to call his sister-in-law and get her to come to Tamoga. At first we doubted the story that Señorita Serena, the operator, gave us. (She's completely senile and about to retire). We thought she was trying to sell us another of her fantasies, one of those incredible, grotesque rumors she gets into her head when she has one of her telephonic spiritualist sessions. You see, shortly after her sister died, Señorita Serena discovered that the dead—above all, friends and relatives of hers who had passed over—were trying to get in touch with her through the phone wires. Ever since, she's lived for the lengthy monologues, the weird and wonderful snippets of news that the dead of Tamoga offer her. She was encouraged partly by superstition and popular

18

beliefs, but above all by the parish priest, Father Lozano, who once told his congregation in a memorable, moving sermon that he saw no reason why souls in purgatory shouldn't have recourse to modern means of communication.

That was why we didn't believe her. We thought it was another of her crazy ideas when she told us Mortes had been in the office that night, and had placed a long-distance call. "It was already very late, and I was saying my last prayers, though I don't know the exact time, when I heard flip-flop, the sound of footsteps on the stairs. Then, *ora pro nobis*, he came in like a phantom, whiter than the wall and soaked right through, dripping from head to toe, his hair plastered down over his eyes. He was groping along with his hands out in front of him, his hands and arms were covered in mud. He was a real sight to see," said Señorita Serena in her melodramatic style. "He could hardly speak, he made gurgling noises and sounded as though he was choking on every word. I thought he was a drunk who was going to throw up in front of me," she added.

"Srreaally uuurgen," he stammered. Later she, Señorita Serena, heard Mortes ask for someone to come and join him in Tamoga: ". . . ope you . . . com and . . . ook me in the eye and . . . ell me . . . ace to . . . ace you don . . . ove me," he said, his voice echoing down the line. From the far end came a continuous sobbing and then a woman's voice saying desperately, "Wait wait wait," before the line went dead.

But all this was later confirmed by the woman (Mortes's sister-in-law) when she came to Tamoga.

We also learned that he (Mortes) was in the Mezquita café. At around ten, Barbosa, the waiter there, saw him cross the red earth courtyard, carefully stepping around the puddles, come to a halt to examine the deserted pergola with the chairs piled against the wall, uncertain or disoriented for a second or two, then push open the back door to the café and peer in at the almost completely empty room. At that moment the only customer was Doña María, from the old people's home. As usual at that time of night, Barbosa was arguing with her, refusing to serve her the second drink she invariably ended up ordering. "What can I get you?" the barman asked him. Tired or distracted, Mortes stared at the old woman, at the waiter's dirty white jacket, then at the row of bottles behind the bar. "I don't know," he said, leaning on the counter. "Yes, let me have a cognac and a glass of water," he said eventually. At that point Doña María insisted, "Pour me another aniseed," pushing her empty glass to the edge of the bar. (She, the old woman from the home, receives a small pension every month. "My son sends it to me," she repeats proudly, to show us she isn't on her own, that someone remembers her; but by midmonth the money has evaporated or gone down the drain, and then, every day, Barbosa serves her a glass of aniseed he knows he'll never be paid for. It's also likely that Doña María goes to the Mezquita not so much because she needs a drink, even if it is free, but for the pleasure and habit of arguing with the waiter, to see him refuse and then finally give in.)

"Another aniseed," the old woman squawked.

"I said no," Barbosa told us. "I was annoyed she was taking advantage of the stranger being there, figuring I wasn't going to argue or refuse her another drink in front of someone we didn't know."

At that point Mortes himself stepped in: "Serve her the aniseed if that's what she wants. I'll pay." Then Barbosa: "It'll be bad for her. She's already had a glass here, and I bet she had two or three more on the way over." Mortes: "Serve the lady." He bowed his head toward her, either shyly or insolently, leaning forward to study her wrinkled, powder-caked face, her tiny, lifeless eyes, the mangy fox fur hanging from her bony shoulders. He acted the perfect, gallant gentleman. Then he turned back to the barman. "If we're old enough, we get to the point where nothing is bad for us. Anything that lets us go on living is good for us, isn't that right, my dear?" he said, head tilted to one side, his voice low. He leaned back against the bar and listened politely to the old woman's chatter, as if he had already decided to court her.

He listened patiently, pretending to be interested and smiling pleasantly at everything she said, nodding slowly and reassuringly as she explained in a not-altogether-logical fashion that she was in the old-age home to preserve her independence: "My children live far away, and want me to go and live with them. Just imagine, young man, me in their house: it wouldn't be long before my daughters-in-law and I were at each other's throats. No, no . . ." she said, giving the excuse she had repeated so often she had come to believe it herself, entirely taken in by the convincing way she told it: "I live alone to honor the memory of my husband, there wasn't a man more in love in all the world. Many evenings after work he would say to me: *Ma, let's go and enjoy ourselves*, and we'd go out to dance. He really loved Viennese waltzes and French champagne. He could dance and still drink his glass down, what he called the champagne waltz. That's all there is for me, young man, the memory of my husband."

At this Mortes inclined his head once more: "Madame, would you do me the honor of accompanying me to the dance so that I can buy you a glass of champagne?"

"He was a comedian," said Barbosa, scandalized. "Either he was making fun of her or he wasn't right in the head."

"He was a gentleman, the first gentleman to set foot in Tamoga," the old woman retorted.

It is worth recalling Mortes's brief, unreal appearance at the Terranova. With the by now quite tipsy woman on his arm, he solemnly rounded off the final act in his farce of love and compassion. As he led her over to a table, he tried to make the sailors and whores show her some respect, then he called out firmly for a bottle of French champagne, although in the end he had to settle for one from Catalonia. He raised his glass in a toast with her, smiling through the smoke and ignoring the deafening noise of the music and laughter. He went up to the bar and whispered in the barman's ear, slipping him a banknote while he was talking. Not wanting to look into the man's alarmed face, Mortes asked him to take off the boring, vulgar chachacha and put on a waltz instead. It's easy to say the words, but impossible to recreate the grotesque tenderness, the fantastical atmosphere of the scene. Slowly and considerately, Mortes led the old woman out onto the dance floor, gently put his arm around her waist, and began to move to the rhythm of the music. Clumsily at first, but increasingly light-footed, aerial even, her feet hardly touching the floor, his partner let him guide her, allowed herself to be carried away by the music, an ecstatic smile on her face and her eyes tightly closed, in the arms of this serious, ceremonious, Chaplinesque man, who turned and turned ever more quickly while in the suffocating gloom of the Terranova the whores and other clients looked on in astonishment, defending themselves with laughter and admiration, rubbing their eyes and asking themselves if what they were seeing was real, if they would be able to tell the story the next day when they had sobered up, if anyone would believe them.

That was all. This was the last that was seen of Mortes, although afterwards Doña María told her group of admiring, sighing old ladies that he had accompanied her to the door of the old-age home and said by way of farewell: "Allow me to kiss you on the forehead, as though you were my mother or my first girlfriend, in memory of tonight." And, after all that had gone before, we might well believe it—fundamentally, it wouldn't be a lie, even if it never happened.

There's nothing else now except to draw this incomplete story to its close. We heard nothing more about him, Mortes, until the woman, a blonde with a drawn, scared-looking face, came and asked after him at the London Hotel. She arrived on the same train as Mortes had done two days before, just in time to identify the body, the corpse covered in seaweed that had been washed up a few hours earlier on the beach at Puerto Angra. She accepted the news with great dignity, but would not accept what Inspector Cardona told her about Mortes's death. She said it was impossible that he would have committed suicide now, precisely when he had told her to come to him, that they were going to live together. She seemed proud of his love, which was all she had left. She stared at his body stretched out on the marble slab in the morgue, then kissed his face, eaten away by crabs. She stroked the hair plastered down on his forehead, stared some more, kissed his empty eye sockets, pressed her lips to his ear and whispered something to him, then caressed him again until she felt the inspector's kind hand on her shoulder. She turned to face him, and said in her proud, terse way: "It must have been an accident, Inspector. There's no other explanation."

Possibly there is no other explanation, or we could accept several, really—any one will do. Possibly the ambiguous hypothesis Doctor Rey the pathologist put forward is the most plausible:

"This man could have committed suicide or had an accident, slipping and falling into the water. I don't know. Either way could have accounted for his drowning," Doctor Rey told the inspector in his concise manner. "What I do know is that he was condemned to die: he had lung cancer. I don't know if he knew this or had come to suspect it, even though it seems logical to suppose he had. Perhaps that's why he came to Tamoga (don't pay too much attention to what I'm saying, Inspector). Because, though it may be hard to live in this town of Tamoga, it's a better place than anywhere to come to die."

II.

THE SHADOWS

She was awakened by the acrid smell of smoke. She had fallen asleep staring at a portrait of her husband. For more than half a century, Doña Sacramento Andreini had spent her life looking at old family photographs. She scarcely did anything else. Shut up almost always in her bedroom, twice a day she walked laboriously from her bed to the armchair next to the table with the pan of hot coals underneath. Even this was torture for her stiff joints. She felt increasingly weak and clumsy. After peering at any photo for a short while, she would start to nod off. Once, even the previous winter, she had sat for hours in a trance staring at one of the many photographs of her husband. Now she felt tired almost at once.

As night fell she had fallen asleep in the chair, clutching a portrait of her husband Salvador. When she opened her eyes, through her tears she saw the smoke rising from the cloth covering the brazier. As she tried to get up, the bones in her arms and legs crackled like logs on a fire. She could not move. She was pinioned, as if her dry, bony body had become nailed to the chair after so many hours resting there. Her legs had gone to sleep. From the window at the far end of the room she could see the street and the dark grove of trees in the park. She struggled in the chair for a few moments, but could not stand up. The heavy album of portraits she pored over every afternoon fell from her lap.

"Salvador," she moaned weakly, "Salvador, where are you?"

Through the clouds of smoke she could see him, impeccably dressed in his gray flannel suit and silk waistcoat with black polka dots, staring at her wide-eyed from a blurred distance, his hair smoothed down over his forehead. He stood there looking on scornfully, smiling as she clutched his portrait between her fingers, still unable to rise from her chair. She started to cough; her eyes streamed with tears. She felt as though she was starting to suffocate. Her small, scrawny head swung to and fro like a pendulum above her stiff upright body. By now she was covered in smoke, her eyes staring through the gloom, stupefied, like two holes burned in a face as dusty and faded as parchment.

She was very old. No one knew exactly how old. Her exact age was a mystery, and was often a talking point for the inhabitants of Tamoga. Some people swore Doña Sacramento Andreini must be more than a hundred; others said she was only a little over eighty, although they had no doubt she would reach a hundred, given that she was completely crazy and had an iron constitution.

Like a nun in a cloistered order, she had buried herself alive in the house bought by her father (a trader who had amassed a small fortune in Cuba at the end of the nineteenth century) when he returned to Tamoga and decided to live quietly off of his investments. No work had been done for many years on the dilapidated house, which was situated opposite the Alameda, its cracked, ivy-clad walls miraculously held upright by the two adjacent buildings.

Occasionally it was possible to spot a white, blurred face moving briefly behind the lace curtains of the upper story; the silhouette of a bird perched on high keeping watch over the hustle and bustle in the park. The oldest inhabitants of the town remembered the few occasions they had seen her, years before, walking along the streets or going into stores, as historic events.

Following the death of her faithful servant Escolástica several years earlier, Doña Sacramento had refused to employ a new maid—in part out of loyalty to her old one, but mostly out of a maniacal terror regarding change and anything new. Escolática's niece—a skinny, prematurely aged woman whose legs were streaked blue with varicose veins—came in to make her meals twice a day. In spite of her willingness to try and keep the house from falling to pieces, she was never allowed any further than the kitchen. One day when she offered to clean the bedrooms, Doña Sacramento flew into a rage and forbade her to as much as open any doors. The house was a sacred place that no one was permitted to enter after Escolástica's death. There was a lengthy corridor between the kitchen and the bedroom where Doña Sacramento shut herself in to call up her shadows. It was her sanctuary.

After luncheon she would sit in the velvet armchair by the window and stay there until nightfall. With solemn, tranquil gestures she would silently lay out the portraits on the table with the brazier, arranging them as meticulously as though she was playing solitaire, with all the skill of a fortune-teller. She would place the figures side by side, bring the faces close to one another, then move them apart. The ceremony of nostalgia. Her tiny, feeble body, no bigger than an eight-year-old child's, remained upright in the chair while her slippered feet hung down inside the rug to catch the warmth from the brazier, which was lit both winter and summer. Her diminutive head, topped by a black velvet coif, bent and rose rapidly above the photographs with the jerky movements of a bird pecking at a tabletop. Her wizened, scaly hands dexterously shuffled the portraits. She opened and closed her eyes in ecstasy. She would bring her face up close to each portrait and study it, purring with delight. She pressed her thin mouth, livid as a scar, against the photographs, devotedly kissing the sepia-colored faces. She tried to remember when they had been taken, to conjure up the scene. By the end she was exhausted, panting. Her delirium kept her awake, in a state of beatific joy.

She had lost her reason. Everyone knew she was mad, even before the day, in the previous decade, when the mayor and three teachers from Tamoga had gone to talk to her about the construction of a new school. The plan was to build it on a piece of land at the entrance to the town, near the power station. The land belonged to Doña Sacramento Andreini, and its only apparent use was to offer a refuge at night for courting couples desperate to find a secluded spot. The mayor and a delegation of schoolteachers went to visit Doña Sacramento with an offer to buy it. Escolástica, who was almost as small and as wrinkled as her mistress, showed them straight into the old woman's bedroom.

"Forgive me," said Doña Sacramento, without getting up from her chair. "I hardly ever leave my room these days."

She sat there stiffly, dressed in black from top to toe, her head turned calmly toward them in the doorway.

The room was filled with a sour smell mixed with eau de cologne and camphor.

"Please be so good as to sit down—over there, on the sofa," they heard a hoarse but friendly voice call out.

Bewildered, they looked around the dark, dusty room so full of junk they could hardly manage a step without tripping over something: taking in the flaking pink walls; the crystal chandelier; the big mirror with the speckled mercury back; the iron headboard and its gilded brass lilies; the plaster Sacred Heart; the night table crammed with prints, portraits in decorated tin frames, figures of saints; the dressing table full of pots and cardboard boxes; the worn-down carpet; the branched bedside light covered in verdigris; the threadbare, dusty sofa; the shiny, moth-eaten rugs; the faded curtains; the brazier table with its worn green rugs; and, in a corner, the enormous heart-shaped scarlet pincushion dotted with needles, and the red armchair from where a waxen face was staring at them.

As they tried to explain the reason for their visit, they sensed that even though the old woman was looking at them unblinkingly, she was not paying the slightest attention to what they were saying, and had not even heard their offer, the proposal to buy the empty piece of land. The tiny, skull-like head rocked gently to and fro the whole time, as if she was agreeing to their words, yet the eyes, fixed in the gloom, seemed to be staring into space. It was obvious that she was somewhere else.

They outlined the matter in great detail, then stared at the self-absorbed face of the old woman, waiting for her reply.

"It's not for sale," she said at length. "I'm not thinking of selling any property."

"You don't have to give your reply right now," said the mayor. "We can come back in a few days' time."

Rigid, she still sat in her chair, studying them absently. Then she crossed her hands in her lap and looked up at the ceiling. The four men followed the direction of her birdlike head. They were still surveying the stucco branches and flowers decorating the high ceiling when they heard her voice again, calm and collected.

"In any case, you need to speak to Salvador," she said. "He's the one who looks after our business affairs."

Taken by surprise, they shifted uneasily in their seats. They thought they must have misheard, until her faint but perfectly clear voice repeated:

"Talk to my husband."

More than half a century earlier, Doña Sacramento Andreini had married a clerk she met by chance at a carnival ball. His name was Salvador Peña, and he was a bookkeeper in a firm of maize exporters in Puerto Angra. In those days he was an elegant young man, with a pleasant face and clear-cut features, although the excessive care he took over his clothes, as well as his love of poetry, had led to rumors about him being effeminate. None of this ever reached the ears of Sacramento Andreini, who would not have given them any credence anyway. She met him at a Society of Arts dance she had been obliged to attend as guest of honor because her father, old man Andreini, had recently presented the society (made up mostly of artisans) with the billiard table and all the furniture for the games room in their club.

That night, just as she was beginning to get bored, she saw Salvador Peña crossing the throng toward her. She was dazzled. As she danced with the only man she ever loved, oblivious to the noise from the out-of-tune orchestra, Sacramento Andreini thought fearfully of the ten years she had been wasting away in Tamoga without ever having seen the handsomest beau in all the world.

Afterward, several months afterward, her father died.

"Now she'll have to observe the two years of mourning and reclusion that are the custom in Tamoga," some of us said, "and by the time she can appear in public again she'll be an old maid."

They were wrong. Sacramento Andreini shut herself away in her house for two years, but did not give up on her efforts to win Salvador Peña. On the contrary, it was all much easier for her now. A fortnight after her father's funeral, she sent Salvador a note inviting him to pay her a visit. She had no need to go out, because she could make him love her far more easily at home, with no witnesses or company to disturb them. After that first visit, Salvador Peña would cross the threshold of Sacramento Andreini's house punctually at five every Sunday, despite the prying, scandalized eyes of the neighbors behind the net curtains of the houses across the way.

Two years later, they were married. Salvador Peña moved into his wife's house and quit his job (the whole town thought he had only married to escape the boredom of sitting at a dusty desk jotting down the number of bushels of maize leaving the port destined for Ireland) in order to administrate his wife's fortune in the rare moments he wasn't enjoying himself with his friends at the club or playing poker. In fact, his passion for gambling began later: a year after their wedding. The initiator, the promoter of this card-playing sickness in Tamoga, was a man called Blain, a mysterious stranger who very soon became rich. Many years later, the local priest Father Cándido Lozano identified him as the devil, due to his extraordinary likeness to the fallen angel at Saint Michael's feet in the old polychrome statue at the parish church.

At that time, Blain and his victims used to meet until the early hours in the abandoned room on the top floor of the social club. Salvador Peña was one of Blain's most assiduous victims. Perhaps he was tempted by the possibility of making money thanks to the simple and in no way tiring task of moving his fingers and throwing cards onto a table. The fact is that by the time he began to discover—if he ever did discover—that it was not so easy to win as he had imagined at the start, his wife's fortune had already considerably dwindled. And possibly it was his desire for revenge, the rage and desperation he felt at seeing how Lady Luck smiled on Blain night after night, that drove him to carry on gambling. Of course, until then he had not had to pay out a penny, because Blain was generous enough to accept the signature of any loser at the bottom of an IOU, provided he had some property to offer as guarantee.

Although Sacramento Andreini didn't ever seem to be aware of what was going on in Tamoga, the rumors about her husband's financial recklessness finally reached her ears. The whole town figured that Blain must be hypnotizing his gambling companions somehow, because not only did they never spot any of the tricks he must have been employing to give his luck a helping hand, but they quietly allowed themselves to be fleeced night after night in the vain hope that they would win it all back the next evening.

One night, as he was coming home from the club, Salvador saw the top floor lights of his house were on. He guessed his wife must have learned that half her capital had been lost on a green baize table due to the quirks of chance.

He climbed the stairs slowly, resigned to facing a scene. He was mistaken. When he opened the bedroom door, he heard his wife's calm voice:

"Salvador."

She was standing in the middle of the room, wearing a dressing gown that was far too big for her slight form. She looked him up and down serenely. Still standing in the doorway, he heard her say in an equally relaxed voice:

"I don't care if you gamble. I don't want to know anything about your vices. What upsets me is that you allow someone to steal the money."

"*Your* money," he cried, striding over to confront her. "That's what this is about, isn't it?"

She smiled, knowing then she had won.

"No," she said. "It's all yours. I went to the bank this morning and put it all in your name."

Salvador didn't move. He shot a proud, furious look at the tiny woman in front of him, with her red-rimmed, glittering eyes. Then he turned his back on her and went over to the bed.

"Well, I think it's time to go to sleep," was all he said.

Later—several hours later—she was woken by the crash of a gunshot. Her husband had a neat hole in his temple and seemed to be sleeping peacefully, his head buried in his pillow.

No one ever found out why he had committed suicide, still less why he had chosen to die this way, in the marriage bed alongside his wife. A mystery. It was also a mystery that the gun he used to blow his brains out (an outsize revolver that had belonged to old man Andreini) turned up several yards from his body, in the middle of the carpet, as if after pulling the trigger he had thrown it away disdainfully like a useless bit of rag.

Following her husband's funeral, Doña Sacramento Andreini never left her house again. The only clues the inhabitants of Tamoga had that she still existed were when they occasionally caught a fleeting glimpse of her pasty face behind the windows of the old house by the Alameda, or else because Doctor Lago—a distant relative of hers—called on her whenever she had any aches and pains.

The next time she left her home, many years later, she did so feet first, in a coffin. By the time the neighbors, alarmed at the dense clouds of smoke billowing through her windows, had broken into the house, there was nothing they could do for her. The charred remains of the old woman were carried to the cemetery in such a small box that if the coffin hadn't been black, everyone would have thought it was an infant who had died. Those who took a last look at Doña Sacramento's corpse said that it looked like a small, crumpled doll covered with flowers. That was the first impression they got when they saw the old woman at the chapel of rest.

On the way back from her burial, someone said—without intending it as a joke—that in the cemetery Doña Sacramento Andreini would have more company than she'd ever enjoyed in the previous hundred years.

III.

PALONZO

Do you remember the town idiot, Palonzo? A fat man with a toad's face, his flabby cheeks rough with beard, his slack mouth full of black, rotten teeth. Bowlegged, always shoeless, with swollen, misshapen feet. That was how we last saw him, clinging the whole day to the barred window before he was taken far away, off to the capital. Preventive detention. Half the town paraded around the square outside the jail: the women screeching insults, egging on the men, who in turn stared threateningly at the prisoner. All the while Palonzo stood there impassive, drooling, an expression of complete innocence on his vacant, placid face. All those people, the townspeople, anxious to be rid of this abomination. Did they really think he was guilty?

Better to dig deep in memory, to tell the story from "once upon a time" before it falls into oblivion. Yes? Then listen while I tell it.

Ever since he was a child, they called him that: Palonzo. No one in the town knew what his real name was, the one he was baptized with. He had no known family (although there were stories, possibly invented—they must have reached even you); after being abandoned at birth he was everyone's son. The older townspeople surely remember it: how early one winter's morning that bundle of rags appeared—a feeble, shivering wail—in the orphanage gateway.

He grew up like an animal without a master: suspicious, solitary, filthy, covered in pustules. From an early age it was obvious he was a cretin, with no glimmer of lucidity, a raving idiot, a half-wit. Even when he was older, he went around with his privates hanging out, oblivious to smacks or bitter words, but also to any friendly gesture, any real kindness, ignoring all taunts, slippery as an eel, shamelessly relieving himself in full sight of everyone. An offense, a real embarrassment to the town. A calamity. He grew to be big and fat, blubbery, despite the fact that he liked to eat with the mongrel dogs in the street, fighting over bones and scraps in the trash. Growling to fight them off. That's how he always was: filthy, repugnant, bare limbs beneath his rags always stiff with dirt from rolling in the dust or wet grass, sleeping anywhere—in sheds or caves, under the stars if the weather was fine. He was dumb, and spoke only in grunts, rough noises, gargling sounds, absorbed in his own world (do you remember his gentle, vacant grin?). He was worse than useless, not like Maluco, another of our holy innocents, who although he likes to race in front of the town band making faces, is still capable of plowing, chopping wood, running simple errands, or carrying the cross in processions.

Palonzo was only good for his solitary wandering, unfettered and without obligations, needing only the minimum, free and untamed under the sun. Yet some took pity on him: occasionally they gave him their old clothes, offered him food or a little charity. Palonzo accepted everything, agreeing offhandedly without acknowledging the gesture. He liked begging for its own sake. He would stretch out his grimy hand at the church door, begging money from strangers, panting like a hunting dog, simply for the pleasure of hearing the chink of the coin, of feeling its cold hardness between his fingers, overjoyed at the tinkling sound but completely unaware of the use or value of money.

The town saw him grow into a man. He must have been around thirty—you can do the math—when the terrible event occurred: something never before seen in our town. He looked older because of his disheveled, ragged appearance, like a jungle creature with his mud-streaked skin and wolflike gaze.

At the time, nobody thought twice about it when Luzdivina, the old woman who cleaned out cesspits to sell manure, took him in and tried to look after him. She gave him food and a roof over his head, helped him live like a human being. No one was surprised. Nothing could revolt a woman like her: dark-skinned, skeletal, rachitic, always living surrounded by filth. Possibly they told themselves by way of explanation that she felt lonely now that she was growing old, living in her hut in a patch of wasteland on the outskirts of town, so she took in Palonzo like a stray dog, to have company while she was alive, and to receive her dying glance. She used to call out to him, smiling when he came to her, greeting him from afar with a shout of "Son!" That's what she called him, in a loving way. He was Son, that was his only name. That old woman lovingkinded him. Sometimes Palonzo would let her lead him, mounted on her longhaired pony, while she walked alongside. They went down to the beach to collect seaweed. Later they would come back into town: he would still be on the horse's back, sitting on the green bundles, and she would be in front, stooped over, leading them. That was how they passed through the town: strange and distant figures.

Yet it didn't occur to the townspeople that the old woman Luzdivina might be consumed by a secret remorse, some ancient sin; that she might be carrying out her maternal mission to clear her conscience. Surely it wasn't an act of expiation in her old age? Some dim and distant memory? A vague likeness between them, did anyone make the connection? A might-have-been?

And yet, like everyone else, Luzdivina had been young once. She hadn't been ugly, either—she'd had a desirable body, and had known many men in her youth, without shame: thirty years ago—just ask—she had been pointed out as a tramp by the decent people in town. It's even said she had been about to take a husband, someone called Damián, who was a good sort, until he was beaten to death in the hills by three woodsmen, criminals still at large today because of lack of proof (prisoners of God's justice). She, Luzdivina, was left completely destitute and several months pregnant. She gave birth alone on top of the dungheap, cutting the cord of life with her teeth, brave woman. The child: stillborn? Dead a few days later? Abandoned at an early age? No one ever knew. Hence the dreadful suspicion, the reasonable doubt.

So everyone accepted the change, without apparent surprise, secretly relieved that they were free of all responsibility toward that lumbering, doltish man now being looked after by old Luzdivina. But at the start of it all, of the horrific event, something else happened. Does the horror allow for an explanation? Can anyone wash their hands of it?

It was during this period that they closed the houses on this bank of the river, the ones inside the town boundaries. The houses of ill repute, I mean, made of brick, with tin roofs, and with women's clothing—pink or pale blue underwear—hung out to dry on lines outside the doors, waving like insolent banners in the breeze. Leaving school in the afternoon, the town kids were in the habit of running down there to spy on the women from the long grass—women in their carelessly tied dressing-gowns, some of them half-naked—then, as soon as they caught a glimpse of them, the kids would race off, hearts in their mouths, pursued by stones and insults: the fascination of the forbidden, never-to-be-forgotten images. Those women—most of them fat, prematurely aged in their prime, nearly all of them with gold teeth that gave them glittering smiles—had to leave their realm, found themselves forced to scatter. Not that they left the town: they had their faithful, long-standing clients, but from then on they lived a semiclandestine existence, officiating discreetly without the previous celebrations and uproar. But on Saturday nights the men of the town—try to remember—missed all the activity, the happy voices, the singing, the brief quarrels drowned in alcohol, missed letting off steam, the noisy cheerfulness in the brightly lit smoky rooms of the shacks down by the river. The constant to-ing and fro-ing of the women as they dragged the men to their rooms at the bottom of the yard, consoling them for the lives they led, drinking with them, sharing their moments of release. As time dragged mournfully by, they remembered those nights of freedom. Corisco, a wily Portuguese who always had an eye for business, must have seen the possibilities right away: he could sniff out an opportunity from miles off, and was completely unscrupulous. Word soon got around: it was an open secret, repeated everywhere: there was a new way to spend your pay having some fun. Every Saturday night in his store, Corisco organized parties like the old ones. Wine and women in abundance. During the day, Corisco's van brought two or three women from the city, and by nightfall they were set up in his store. The locals started to appear out of darkened streets in the center of town, pretending sheepishly they were headed in no particular direction; they knocked on the door at the back of the store, next to the garage, then went in cautiously, without saying a word but with complicit smiles on their faces. Corisco lined the men up in double file, made sure they paid in advance—cash in hand, fixed price, no discounts—and saw that none of them overstayed their time. Stretched out on sacks, the two or three women received the attentions of the excited crowd of men with calm efficiency and mechanical gestures. Soon, however, this discipline was relaxed: shouts, loving giggles, and heady party sounds reached the street and scandalized the entire neighborhood. In a back room, card games were arranged that lasted all night, every hand hotly disputed.

Everything is known in this town. The authorities were in on the secret, turned a blind eye. Because they stood to make a little money? Almost certainly—bribes and gifts from Corisco.

One joyous Saturday night, Palonzo arrived. Led there by the devil? It was a memorable entrance.

"Let's see if we can get him in the mood," someone shouted in fun.

A new, unexpected source of entertainment. People started to bet on Palonzo's performance. Villagers came from all around: workers from the pottery factory, as well as those from the mines, and the fishermen from Puerto Angra; people from all over, attracted as though by a magnet. Palonzo became famous. It was stupefying. A moron who could exhaust all three women at once, could carry on and on, panting away. They placed more and more extravagant bets on him—he was beyond human. Those sweaty men, their eyes bright with alcohol, couldn't believe what they saw. No trickery: just brute strength. The bets grew larger, serious. Every Saturday they brought Palonzo in, the main attraction. They surrounded him, pushing and pulling impatiently, as if they were watching a close, arduous fight. They say that when he saw the women his face would light up; he was radiant, knowing full well what was expected of him; wanting them all to admire him? In his lust? Out of all control, he threw himself on the women, baring his teeth, tearing at them passionately, howling with love, again and again, beside himself with pleasure, drooling placidly, never-ending.

But soon they all started to tire of Palonzo. They shooed him away, forbade him to come into the store. They threw him a few coins from the doorway; drove him off. Perhaps because they were bored with the same show each time, because there were new distractions, new kinds of bets. Palonzo and his bestial prowess were no longer needed: the customers already knew everything he had to offer. They invented new tricks—fresh, spiteful ways of speculating. Did you hear about the mare races? I see you're smiling. This is a true story. The women—two or three fat ones, brought in from the city—were on all fours, naked, their breasts hanging down, while they were ridden by heavy fellows like Soto and José-Alberto. They spurred them on like jockeys while they scuttled madly across the dirt floor to reach the finish, the counter at the far end. There were different prizes, and lewd encouragement from the spectators.

Palonzo was forgotten, a nostalgic beggar in their memories. He was strictly forbidden to set foot in the store. He was an old joke.

Couldn't they see how he roamed around at nightfall, sniffing for a female, his blood up?

The first incident caused only laughter and sarcasm. One Saturday, Señorita Rosario, the organist, was on her way home after Mass, walking along Calleja del Convento, behind the church, when she heard the roar in the darkness she was terrified. At first she didn't know what to do: stood there quaking, petrified with fear. Then she saw the dark demon, the enormous shadow of Palonzo, grunting as he lumbered toward her, arms open wide. She finally managed to run for it, crying for help between her squeaks of terror, rousing the neighbors. Still, no one bothered too much about an old maid's fears.

But didn't anyone notice—somebody must have—how Palonzo looked at women, all women, even little girls, sighing and salivating? He devoured them with his eyes when they came out of school, girls in short skirts, their bodies just starting to bud. He watched them playing, the funangames at recess, their pink thighs as they skipped rope. Did he really still seem harmless? Was nobody worried about any possible disaster?

When it came, the offense was unexpected, the product of a very disturbed mind: the atrocious idea of uncovering the female in old Luzdivina, Palonzo's new and only mother.

This also happened one Saturday, at night, although in the town nothing was known about it until a day and a half later, when the old woman was discovered (the alarm was raised by a curious neighbor who had spied in through the window) lying on the floor of her shack, with Palonzo beside her. He had made no attempt to escape, and was completely unaware of what had happened; on all fours with his mind empty. Palonzo, moaning over her body; Luzdivina with her torn black petticoats, her scrawny breasts bare, the white-yellow of her half-naked body, the claw marks on her belly and the deep tooth marks on her neck. Palonzo, a dog watching over its mistress, chewing on cold and shadows, unable to comprehend, crying as he had done thirty years earlier, utter confusion: beloved mother-wife, lost next to her, cryhowling. To wake her from her eternal sleep? To bring her back? Moaning his pain? Howling at death? Think about it. Did he want to return to his former dwelling place, had he been feeling a great nostalgia for the dark, warm breast from which he was torn? Was he blinded by complete madness? You're educated people; perhaps one of you can explain it.

IV.

HUNTING IN JULY

His name was Celso Castillo and he was a tailor in Tamoga. From early that morning he knew what his fate was to be. There was no doubt that when the journey came to an end—and there couldn't be far to go because the truck had been bumping along a track in the forest for half an hour now—they would blow his head off, exactly as they had done with the seven men and two women whose dead bodies had appeared the previous morning on the outskirts of the town, next to the stone cross opposite the cemetery (the cross that became known from then on as the Bloody Cross) without anyone in Tamoga trying to discover who the killers were.

Still, the fact that they were taking so much trouble, wasting all that time and gasoline—they were a long way from Tamoga and the sea was already hidden behind the hills which rise up from the coastal highway—began to intrigue Castillo. Perhaps that was why hope struggled with fear inside him, so that he told himself again and again without conviction, feeling increasingly numbed and exhausted: "They're not going to kill me. This is a joke, they're just trying to scare me."

Yet he was sufficiently clear-minded (he only had to remember the lunacy that had been unleashed on Tamoga in the previous days of this bloody, crazy summer) to know that the men hadn't taken him all this way just as a joke.

Standing on the back of the truck, he could feel the cool air on his face. The vehicle was swaying as it went along the narrow dirt road, leaving in its wake a thick cloud of reddish dust that floated in the still July morning. On both sides the pine-tree trunks quickly closed into a wall. He stared intently at the way shadows from the branches darkened the faces of the men guarding him.

He had a wild look to him, Castillo. He was thin, on the tall side, with strong shoulders. His black curly hair sat like a cap almost down to the dark line of his brow. His unshaven face was angular and dark; his shadowy, moist eyes were close-set; his big mouth framed by deep lines in its corners. He was thirty-three the previous winter, but looked ten years older. Like most of the tailors in Tamoga, he was lame. When he walked he did so with grotesque agility, dragging his left foot perpendicular to the right one. He was wearing a dirty, crumpled blue suit, a waistcoat, and a collarless white shirt that was undone and showed the blackish fuzz on his chest.

Now he was standing on the back of the truck, guarded by three men. He didn't understand a thing, and thought of death with the same sense of disbelief and helplessness that those gunned down outside the cemetery must have felt the previous day. He was so stunned that every so often his stupor managed to anesthetize him. Fear had drained his face of color. He felt drowsy and weak, so strange that his legs were like a rag doll's. It was as if he were shrinking by the minute. In the few moments when fear did not completely cloud his mind, he was overwhelmed by a sense of impotence when he realized with amazement that these men whom he had known all his life, and with whom he had never had the slightest quarrel, had overnight turned into enemies ready to punish him for sins he did not even know he had committed.

They were standing close to him. He stared at them but their faces were only impenetrable masks. When he had tried to talk to them at the start of all this, they had smashed him with their rifle butts. They were either nervous or impatient. The least concerned seemed to be Moreira, a thickset man of fifty, the owner of a soft-drinks factory and of the truck they were riding on. Alongside him were José Benito Lozano, the priest's nephew, a tall, pale youth who could not have been more than eighteen, and Nieto, who ran the kiosk on Plaza Nueva. He was a bad-tempered sort, who liked to drink more than anything else in the world. He had worn strict mourning since the death of his brother (who had apparently committed suicide shortly before this, although almost no one in Tamoga believed it was suicide) and looked like an inconsolable widower, despite the fact that he was past forty and still unmarried.

The three men were carrying shotguns, as if this was a cheerful hunting excursion, although the season wouldn't start for another three months.

Celso Castillo could see the backs of the heads of the other two through the truck's rear window: the driver, a broad-shouldered, corpulent man with a huge, barrel-like belly, was called Soto, and was one of the owners of the Tavares sawmills; next to him sat Doctor Emilio Lago, a lively little fellow better known for his political activities and his admiration for the local big shots than for any medical ability.

The truck had gotten a long way into the wood. They were progressing more and more slowly because the track was a steep, dry streambed full of potholes. All at once the vehicle came to a halt, with a faint gurgling sound. They were in a hollow full of ferns and gorse, almost completely surrounded by peaks. Pallid and solemn, Celso Castillo looked enquiringly at his companions. There was an expression of fear on his face, but also resignation and a strange dignity.

"Get down," they ordered him.

As he was about to jump from the truck, he felt himself being pushed. He thrashed his feet in midair, then fell flat on his face, as though his legs had been taken from under him. He lay facedown on the ground. Perhaps he had fallen because of the push they had given him, or perhaps his clubfoot had made it impossible for him to keep his balance.

The men stood around him. He looked up from where he was lying, making no attempt to sit up. He saw pant cuffs, the gun-metal blue of shotguns; then, higher still, unbelievably high, their impassive faces—all of them known to him and yet all of them so different, transformed. And higher still, above their heads, the trunks and dark tops of the pine trees, swaying gently in the breeze, the clear blue sky and the fiery splendor of dawn.

"Pick him up," he heard someone say.

Two men grabbed him by the armpits, dragged him along a little way, then pulled him violently upright. Until he was standing erect it was as if his body had no skeleton, as if all his limbs had been crushed in the same way as his misshapen foot. He stared at the men, panting for breath.

The one who stood out was a giant with broad, muscular shoulders, wide as a door. This was Soto. He wasn't carrying a gun. He looked half-asleep, with red-rimmed, drooping eyelids. He lumbered across, the others staring at him in silence. When he was a few paces away from Celso Castillo, he halted. He was wearing a pair of corduroy trousers and a suede jacket with resin stains. He took a revolver out of one of the bulky pockets, looked at it for a few moments as though trying to identify what he had in the palm of his hand, weighed it carefully, then wrapped his fingers around it, laughing quietly, the way he did when he told one of his jokes in the sawmill during the lunch break. Slowly raising his right arm, he pushed the gun barrel against Celso Castillo's chest. The tailor stood facing him meekly. He could feel the pressure against his skin and instinctively flinched. Scared, he fixed his gaze on Soto's half-closed eyes in his faintly smiling face. He looked at the others, standing in a semicircle around him. They seemed amused, expectant. He felt a heavy blow to his chest and dug in his heels to stop himself falling over backwards. He waited for the next assault. Soto hit him again with the revolver.

"Run, Castillo," he told him. "You're going to get a chance no Red deserves."

Two hours earlier, Celso Castillo had been having a nightmare. He hadn't spent a good night, constantly disturbed by the solemn chimes of the clock in the main square. At five in the morning, just as he was falling asleep, his wife woke him. Celso Castillo opened his eyes, scratched his unshaven chin, then murmured thickly: "I dreamed a seagull was picking at my entrails." Relieved to discover it was only a dream, he smiled and turned to face the wall.

"Did you hear that noise?" his wife asked, shaking his shoulders. "Someone's trying to get in."

"No," he replied. "It must be a dog rummaging in the garbage can."

He listened for a while. After several minutes' complete silence, just as he was about to fall asleep again, he heard a noise at the street door. He sat upright in bed.

"Switch the light on," he told his wife.

She fumbled clumsily by the bedside until she found the light switch. The bulb, dangling from the ceiling by a fuzzy cable, filled the room with a yellowish glow. It was a poor bedroom, with whitewashed walls and planks on the floor that had often been patched up. There was an iron double bed, a cupboard, two chairs piled high with clothes, and a small trundle bed where a boy of around seven was sleeping. The room was at the rear of the house, and was linked at the back to the kitchen, with a narrow, dank courtyard outside. The tailor's shop was on the far side of the courtyard: it was spacious, and had a door and a window looking out onto Plaza Nueva.

His wife got out of bed, terrified. She was blonde, with a broad, beautiful face. Her name was Adoración and had been married to the tailor Castillo for eight years. Before that she had been the mistress of Daniel Tavares, one of the main landowners in the region. Following her marriage, she forgot her amatory generosity (to the despair of the males of Tamoga, including the proud Tavares) and substituted strict fidelity for her previous way of life, the days when she used to dance naked in one of the shacks down by the river, satisfying one by one the crowd of men who formed anxious, impatient lines to be with her.

Her wedding to the tailor Castillo caused a great commotion among the many men who had taken their turn with her on Saturday nights.

The couple had a child, a thin, dark-skinned boy with the same sad, deep-set eyes as Celso Castillo, although this wasn't sufficient to dispel the widespread rumor that Adoración was already carrying Tavares's baby in her belly when she married the tailor.

Castillo and his wife heard a long cracking sound, as if someone was trying to lever open the front door from outside.

"It must be Adriano," said the woman, looking over at her husband who was running to the middle of the bedroom in his underwear.

"Don't talk nonsense," he replied, hurriedly pulling on his trousers.

He was frightened. His wife's idea sent a shiver down his spine. Although everyone in the town knew he hadn't been on speaking terms with his brother Adriano for years, Celso Castillo had been anxious ever since—a week earlier—Adriano had tried to blow up the door to the jail where the Republican authorities were locked up. It was a reckless undertaking, poorly executed, but Adriano Castillo had escaped after killing two Civil Guards. The word was that he was in the hills organizing a resistance, planning to come and attack the whole town.

When news of the military rebellion reached Tamoga, two days after it had happened, the peasants from the surrounding area came down to the town in carts or on foot, some of them bringing their wives. A sad kind of pilgrimage. When they gathered in the Campo de la Feria, they found that all the exits were blocked, and they were mown down by troops. That same night, the fishermen, dockers, and workmen from the local potteries barricaded themselves in the Casa del Pueblo. For almost two days they fought off the combined attacks of the soldiers and the Civil Guard. Finally the building was set alight, they were forced out. After that, the rebels organized punishment patrols. Right up until the end of that month of July, it was common at night to see the glow of fires in the countryside. When the resistance was finally snuffed out, Tamoga's tiny jail had room for only a quarter of those arrested. The town hall and a school on the outskirts of Tamoga (this school—a mansion surrounded by high walls down by the river—was to be a concentration camp for several years) were turned into prisons. Summary executions soon solved the space problem. New bodies appeared every day, flung by the roadside. The women who used to go down to the public washhouses by the port were greeted one morning by the sight of several corpses floating like fish in the soapy waters of the tanks.

For the inhabitants of Tamoga, the war was an excuse to settle many years of bitter resentment.

Like any other small town, it had always been a place for rumors and gossip, but now the ease and fervor with which true or false news was spread reached unheard-of proportions. Everyone was afraid of everyone; nobody felt safe, because individual responsibility could be extended back to their most distant ancestors.

This was why when he heard his wife mention Adriano, Celso Castillo was filled with a sense of dread.

"If it's Adriano, don't let him in," Adoración shouted as he opened the bedroom door.

"There's no way it can be him," he thought apprehensively as he crossed the yard. He paused for a few moments. He could hear a noise in the tailor's shop. A line of light shone beneath the door. When he went in, he pulled up short, alarmed. First he saw all the bolts of cloth scattered across the floor like giant snakes. Then he saw several men ransacking the cabinets.

"Well, I suppose you haven't hidden him in your bed."

He was so stunned that it was only now, when he heard the voice, that he realized who these people were. Doctor Lago stood in front of him, giving orders:

"Search the rooms at the back," he said.

Soto and Moreira opened the door to the yard. The tailor made to follow them, but José Benito blocked his way, then pushed him back with his gun.

"Sit down," he barked.

Celso Castillo turned slowly until his back was to the door. The doctor pushed him gently toward a wicker chair under the circle of light from the lamp. He studied him silently for a moment, blinking nervously, then placed a hand on Castillo's chest as if he was going to listen to it.

"You wouldn't by any chance know where Adriano is, would you?" he asked.

Celso Castillo shook his head.

"You know I have nothing to do with him," he said in a low voice.

The alarm had faded from his face; all that was left was a look of defeat. Doctor Lago sat down in silence next to him.

A quarter of an hour later, the doctor got up and strode across the room. He paused for a moment with his hand on the doorknob to listen, then made his way across the yard. From the back of the house there came a murmur of voices and the unmistakable, though muffled, sound of a child crying. Moreira and Soto came into the shop. As they did so, Soto gave a sigh and Moreira began to guffaw, until José Benito raised a finger to his lips.

"Come with us, Castillo," said the doctor. He had just come back in, his face flushed.

A truck was standing outside the front door of the shop. As he climbed on board, Celso Castillo heard screams. He couldn't see where they were coming from because he was pushed down on the floor of the back of the truck. "On the floor, dammit," he heard them order, as they kicked him and covered him with a tarpaulin.

When they let him get up, he saw a dusty track and a horizon of trees.

Some time later, when he heard the order to run, he didn't move. He was bewildered, as though he hadn't really understood, even though the words were perfectly clear: "Run, Castillo. You're going to get a chance no Red deserves."

An explosion rang out close to his head. Lead pellets ricocheted against his legs. He had to jump in the air as he zigzagged to try to avoid the volleys. His feet sometimes got snagged in the undergrowth, but he ran nimbly, pursued by the rattle of gunfire and the men's harsh voices. Whenever he jumped, he could hear their laughter. They even stopped shooting for a while as he performed his grotesque dance steps in midair, still running with all his might.

"If I reach the ravine, maybe I'll get away," he thought, feeling the race would never end, that the distance separating him from the ravine was infinite, that his lungs were about to burst, that the air was choking him. The sun was boiling his brain, its rays blinding him. Sweat ran down his face like scalding tears. He jumped and fell into a gorse bush. He pushed himself forward, sinking his hands and arms in the thorny branches. The sweat from his forehead soaked his shirt, already stuck to his skin. When he started to run again he felt a burning sensation in his back and something like the lash of a whip behind his knees. He stumbled, took a few more steps, then leaned against the trunk of a pine tree. At the same moment as he heard the explosion inside his chest, he saw the ravine. It was a high, steep gully. At the bottom there was a big forest. He slid to the ground with a sense of relief. His body slipped quickly across the soft floor of pine needles. He fell down and down.

The wind brought the sound of distant voices. He stood up and examined his wounds through his torn clothes. They weren't serious. There was a steady flow of blood from his chest, but it wasn't a deep wound. He felt light and strong. He bent his arms and legs and found he could move them with ease. He set off running through the wood. The sunlight filtered down through the green vaults like rays through the stained-glass windows of a church.

The earth was damp and pleasantly soft beneath his club foot, even more battered from all his leaping. As he stumbled on, the wood grew darker. A sickly sweet smell rose from the ground and wafted through the air. The dense silence wiped the memory of the explosions and the shouts of his pursuers from his mind.

He ran exuberantly, quickly and agilely, until his ears began to throb. He fell face downwards, feeling his heart thumping against the ground. He pressed his head against the earth, watching an orderly line of ants making for a tree trunk that had fallen across the path. A red, fleshy fungus sticking to the rotten trunk caught his attention. He closed his eyes for a few seconds, until tears began to well up. It was a feeling of relief. His pursuers had lost his trail, and he was all alone, surrounded by silence. With his eyes shut, he was in a darkness that flooded over him like a tide rising up through his body and carrying him off to a deep, warm, sticky cavern.

He did not hear the sound of footsteps when the men came up and saw him slumped underneath a tree at the edge of the ravine. He did not feel the violent kick that turned his body over, or the deafening thunder of the shotguns fired at point-blank range.

V.

THE HOUSE DIVIDED

"Delia!" he shouted, leaning over the top of the dark stairwell.

He stood there for several seconds, paralyzed by astonishment and concern. He called out again to his sister: "Delia!"

There was no reply. All he heard was his own voice echoing around the walls of the entrance hall.

He grabbed the banister, leaning out over the dark stairwell. His hair fell over his eyes as he tried desperately to peer into the darkness. He was having trouble breathing, and his face was flushed from their argument, far more violent and fierce than any before. Motionless, listening for the slightest sound, Horacio Arias wracked his befuddled brain for some idea of what to do next.

He leaned against the rail, which creaked and groaned beneath his colossal weight. He thought to himself without conviction: "She's trying to frighten me. That's why she's not replying." He straightened up and started down the stairs. He walked laboriously, with slow, clumsy movements. Rancor and exasperation gradually gave way to fear.

When he reached the first landing, he told himself firmly: "I have to go downstairs before María Rita arrives." He said this out loud, as though giving himself an order, to force himself to continue down. He wondered if he was brave enough, knowing his sister Delia was waiting for him at the entrance, a terrible expression on her face, just like when he was a little boy and she would shake him by the shoulders if he had been up to some mischief. He didn't want to switch the light on, but fumbled his way down the stairs in darkness, so as not to have to see what he could not avoid seeing once he had stepped off the last stair onto the tiles of the big hall.

"Delia," he called out again, almost in a whisper. This time there was no resentment in his voice, only dismay.

He was big and fat, in poor health, and with a pinched, anxious look about him because of his chronic asthma. He was almost forty, the owner of a draper's shop that was successful enough to allow him to live without any financial worries. He was the last male member of the Arias family, one of the oldest in town, although it had been in sharp decline for more than half a century.

He lived in a two-story house on the corner of Plaza del Ayuntamiento. He shared it with his only sister, Delia. The two of them had inherited the house fifteen years earlier, after the death of their father, a lackluster shopkeeper with far too great a liking for gambling, who in a few years had managed to fritter away a considerable fortune accumulated over several generations. Brother and sister had always lived together, apparently in perfect harmony until María Rita arrived at the start of the previous year. Delia was a vinegary spinster several years older than her brother, accustomed to giving orders and to Horacio's constant submissiveness. That was why it was such news, such a shock to the people of Tamoga, when the old house on Plaza del Ayuntamiento was divided, brother and sister separated. Everyone watched in amazement as from one day to the next two teams of workmen hastily blocked up the main front door, built two staircases and put in two new, independent doors in the narrow façade overlooking the square. It was an absurd division that ruined the harmony of the building.

So the two of them want such a decisive split they won't even meet on the stairs, everyone thought.

It had all begun on a cold, gray day in February almost two years earlier. Horacio had just closed the shop and was sitting at the table with the brazier under it about to set to work sorting out his stamp collection—his favorite pastime on winter evenings— when he saw her for the first time.

"She's the new maid. Her name is María Rita," his sister informed him.

She was standing in the hallway next to Miss Delia, a few steps away from the open living-room door, clutching a small cardboard suitcase to her body. "Good evening," she said in a calm, pleasant voice, depositing the case on the floor and peering into the lighted room. Horacio glanced up from his collection and looked her up and down.

She was very young (she cannot have been more than sixteen): modest and shy. On the thin side, she was poorly dressed in a black mourning skirt and jersey that were already beginning to lose their color. This was the first time she was entering service. She had come from a nearby village with a letter of recommendation from the local priest in which he said she was well brought up, and that her mother had died the previous winter. She had never known her father.

Although the priest's letter did not say so, she also turned out to be extremely hardworking. She worked tirelessly, as if she had set herself the goal of accomplishing as much as three diligent, energetic people. Naturally enough, Delia was as delighted as she was surprised. Horacio on the other hand felt inexplicably restless from the first evening he saw María Rita. It took him more than two months to realize that the cause of his sleepless nights, his irritability, and his endless anxiety, was in fact desire. One night he woke up bewildered from a dream in which María Rita allowed herself to be undressed and then responded to his advances with expert, urgent caresses. Unable to get back to sleep, Horacio lay in the darkness, finally aware that he was being tortured by a secret, reckless passion. He had to accept what he had known from the start, but had been trying to deny all this time: that his anxiety and restlessness were linked to the image of a country girl fixed in his brain ever since the first evening he had seen her, with her suitcase and that meek look in her eyes. "So that's what it is," he told himself, furious and humiliated. "That damned kid, who's half my age; a serving girl, a country bumpkin who isn't even beautiful."

Until that moment he had never desired a woman for more than a few hours, and of course no one whom he couldn't have immediately. His lovemaking had always had the brutal energy of a physical imperative, the impersonal practicality of a commercial transaction.

He got up an hour earlier than usual and dressed quietly, doing his best not to wake his sister, who was asleep in the adjacent bedroom. Without bothering to wash and with his hair unkempt, he went down to the kitchen. The first thing he saw in the gray light of dawn was the dazzling nakedness of a pair of white, well-rounded thighs. He couldn't breathe. María Rita was kneeling on the floor, her body bent forward, furiously scrubbing the kitchen tiles.

"María Rita," he said, struggling to get the words out, quivering with excitement.

She must not have heard him, because she didn't turn her head and kept on scrubbing. He took a step toward her, then stopped, unable to take his eyes off the vibrant, lithe body at his feet. She stood up with a smile and greeted him respectfully: "Good morning, sir." She dried her hands on her apron, went over to the stove, and took off the steaming pot. Horacio collapsed onto a chair, leaned his elbows on the pinewood kitchen table, and didn't move or raise his eyes. He almost dozed off, until he noticed the sharp smell of bleach and soap, and felt her body brush against him. She was wiping the table with a rag. First he saw her wet red hands and bare arms; then, with increasing anxiety, the slight, rhythmic tremble of her breasts under the frayed blouse as she moved to and fro. She went over to the cooker and returned with the coffee-pot and a dish full of slices of fried bread. As she served him coffee, he could feel the persistent pressure of her firm breasts against his back. He didn't budge until she had moved away from him. When she reached the far side of the table, she stared back at him with a placid look in her big, dark eyes as if she was trying to read the reason for his distress in his haggard features.

He was so much on edge that he hardly touched his breakfast. He got up from the table in a rush, crossed the kitchen in two strides, and went out without a word and without looking at her, his mouth set in a firm line, a wild expression on his face.

He spent the rest of the morning behind the counter at his shop, trying in vain to be pleasant to his customers. He went home at lunchtime and, sitting opposite his sister and ignoring her constant chatter, thought he could detect a complicit look in María Rita's eyes, as if the two of them shared a secret. Holding his breath and looking over at his sister in terror, he found that the maid was brushing against him again, although more discreetly than she had done at breakfast. Sometimes he felt the warm palm of her hand as she took away a piece of cutlery; at others, her body pressed against his back when she placed a dish on the table; and again, her breast rubbed against his shoulder when she came to the table. Once Horacio was sure Delia hadn't noticed any of this, he glanced stealthily at the maid: all her movements looked natural and innocent, even when her body stiffened as she cleared away the plates and her smooth, soft forearm almost imperceptibly touched his cheek.

That night as he tossed and turned in bed, suffering a more intense asthma attack than ever before, he again felt an overwhelming desire for her.

Things stayed the same, day after day. More than once he wondered if he was losing his mind, because when he met María Rita's gaze, he thought he could briefly see in her eyes a provocative wink or a flash of cunning. He was in a state of constant anxiety.

Finally, one night, after several weeks of uncertainty, not knowing whether he was suffering from the fantasies of an overheated imagination, the nervous exhaustion caused by his unhinged desire, or was simply the butt of a provocative young woman's joke, he could bear it no longer. He got out of bed determined once and for all to put an end to this prolonged torture. He had been turning back and forth for several hours, unable to sleep as he imagined María Rita's body in the darkness. Stealthily, then, he opened his bedroom door and left the room barefoot, dressed only in his pajamas. Tiptoeing down the dark corridor, he paused for a moment outside the closed door of his sister's room, until he clearly heard her steady breathing from the other side of the door. He crept over to the stairs, trying not to wake her. He fumbled his way up the eight steps leading to the attic, and stopped, breathing heavily, at the first landing in front of a small, unpainted door. Pushing it open, he edged inside, stooping down and trying to find his way in the dark. He bumped into a chair piled high with clothes, almost knocking it over, then realized he was already in the middle of the small room, which had a low, sloping roof. Two steps away from him was an iron bed. By the wall on the right was a washbasin and jug, with a broken piece of mirror above it. As his eyes became used to the darkness, he could make out a mop of black hair on the pillow. He was quivering with cold and apprehension.

"María Rita," he said softly, going over to the bed.

As he called out faintly in the freezing darkness, he remembered the morning he had done the same in the kitchen, and she hadn't heard him. But this time she had.

"At your service," she said.

That was all. She was sitting up in bed, staring at him. There was no sign of surprise or sleep on her face, as if she had been waiting for him. There was a sweet, calm look in her eyes. She had a smile on her lips. She did not recoil or push him away when he sat on the edge of the bed and began to caress and then kiss her with a fraught, desperate aggression. He buried his face in her shoulder as with trembling hands he tried to strip the submissive body beside him. He stretched out avidly, feeling how the exasperation and agonies of a desire built up over the months suddenly slipped away in a languorous spasm. Crushed beneath his bulky body, she let out a low moan when he thrust brutally into her.

From that night on they established a habit, a ritual that lasted several months. When the first light of day filtered in through the tiny window of María Rita's room, Horacio freed himself from her embrace and crept back to his own room just in time to have a quick nap and leave the imprint of his body on his mattress.

One morning as he returned to his room, however, he found Delia sitting on the edge of the bed.

"Sit down a moment."

Dumbstruck, he stood in the doorway, his hand still on the latch. Then he turned to face his sister, looking at her without a word.

"She must leave this house at once. Right now," said Delia. Her voice was firm but she remained calm, scrutinizing her brother. Coldly, disdainfully, she considered his grotesque, forlorn figure, looking more bloated and colossal than ever in his baggy pajamas.

Horacio stared at her blankly, as if he hadn't understood what she had said. Then he held his breath for a few moments, pressed his fists into his hips, opened his mouth without saying a word, hesitating momentarily as if he was just as surprised as anyone by the reply he was about to give, then breathed out heavily and said:

"No."

This was the first time he had dared oppose his sister, and he did so in such a determined, forceful way that it brooked no argument.

Delia blinked several times and raised her eyebrows in scandalized disbelief. She crossed her hands on her chest as if afraid he might attack her, and could only stammer:

"You surely can't mean that . . ."

Stepping back several paces, Horacio raised his arm, pointed to the door, and said in a level voice:

"Please leave. I need to get dressed."

His sister was so astonished she had almost no idea what to say.

"I cannot tolerate this indecency!" she said on her way out. "Keeping a mistress in my own home!"

That was the start of a war of insults and violent arguments that culminated a few weeks later with the division of the house and the separation of brother and sister. Horacio lived with María Rita, completely oblivious to the town gossip, in his half of the house. Miss Delia lived in the other half of the old building on the square, having to put up with the humiliation of being separated from the lovers by nothing more than a thin partition.

Scarcely two years had passed from the day the intruder burst in upon the brother and sister's previously tranquil existence when the women friends who came to visit Delia every afternoon brought her the news. At first she couldn't believe what they told her. She almost spilled the cup of tea she was raising to her lips all down the front of her sternly buttoned black dress. She and her friends were gathered in the reception room, a gloomy place filled with furniture and with imposing portraits of her ancestors lining the walls.

"I hadn't noticed myself, not until today. Her belly's as big as a drum," one of her friends said crudely. "We saw her in the square on our way here, the shameless hussy."

"It's a disgrace. Who would have thought it?" said the other friend. "In a few days they're announcing the wedding banns in church."

"No," Delia moaned, choking on her words. "That wretch . . ."

All at once her face shriveled up. In the narrow slit of her brows, her eyes were like sharp, furious needles. "It's impossible, impossible," she repeated under her breath, her chin on her chest. Visibly taken aback, her lips pressed into a livid furrow, she could not look at her two friends. Heads down over their crocheting, they sneaked stealthy looks at her enraged grimace, perhaps secretly satisfied.

By the time her friends had left, later on in the evening, Delia's mind was made up. She dressed unhurriedly in what had once been her parents' bedroom. "My God," she said with a deep sigh, looking at herself in the mirror. "I have to stop this shameful wedding."

Tall and bony, the black dress emphasized her sallow complexion and the extraordinary fragility of her body. She wore her hair scraped back against the sides of her head, with a helmetlike, copper-colored bun on top. Her face was lined, but her harsh eyes and the knots of muscle at the top of her jaws gave her a stubborn, indomitable look. She washed her hands, carefully soaping and rubbing them together for several minutes, trying to wash away dirt that wasn't there. She always did the same thing, with an attention bordering on obsession. Going back into her bedroom, she put on her black coat, chose a black hat adorned with feathers that she wore only on solemn occasions, and went out into the square. She took a few steps and then, at her most dignified, went in at the front door next to hers. She walked up the stairs calmly but without stopping until she reached the door on the top floor. She paused for a few moments, smoothed down her coat, and tried to get her breath back. She rang the bell once, as firmly as she could. She heard the sound of slow, heavy footsteps coming toward the door, then muffled breathing as though somebody had stopped to listen.

"Open up," she said. "I know you're there."

Horacio appeared in the doorway, a look of surprise and dismay on his face. He stood with one hand on the doorframe, his bulk preventing her from pushing past him.

"So she's got her way with you at last," she screamed at him.

"Be quiet."

"I have no intention of being quiet. You're going to have to listen to everything I say to you."

Horacio took a step toward her, one arm raised. The immense jowls dangling down over his neck puffed up, went scarlet and quivered.

"Go away," he said hoarsely. "Go away. Get out of here once and for all."

There was a lengthy, tense silence. Horacio did not move, his arm still outstretched. He was finding it hard to breathe as he glared at his sister.

She did deign to notice his aggressive gesture, but stared him full in the face, meeting his gaze and trying to intimidate him in return. She could hear the asthmatic crackle of his labored breathing.

"I am not going to allow that woman, that . . ." she began.

Seeing the wild look in her brother's eyes, she took a step backward.

"That harlot," she said, feeling the handrail in the small of her back.

At this, Horacio plunged forward, head down, as though he was going to ram into her. His arm shot out. His hand made contact with something hard and bony, pushed it away from him in disgust, and saw with disbelief the brief fluttering of a monstrous, black-winged bird. It was a moment of utter confusion. He was blinded by the dark beating of wings in front of him, then the vertiginous fall. He heard the cry and almost simultaneously a dry, distant sound as the body crashed onto the tiles of the entrance hall.

The shock paralyzed him. A few seconds later, he peered over the banister, panting for breath.

"Delia!" he shouted, leaning over the top of the dark stairwell.

VI.

SECOND PERSON

How to explain it, the weightlessness, the marvelous feeling of lightness and freedom when you slip into the shadows and the night explodes in a dazzling flash and ten thousand million stars go out, are slowly extinguished in a shudder of ice, then a torrent of sparks dissolves in a glittering burst as you drift aimlessly in the boundless dark. How to explain the feeling of anxiety that grips you at the start, when you think you're becoming lost in a strange but vaguely recognizable place, until finally you discover you are in your own bedroom. Everything is hazy, though; the furniture and objects are bathed in a different light, as if you were looking at them through an out-of-focus lens, but you recognize the double bed with its canopy and carved columns—too showy for your taste, but which you've kept out of a sense of tradition, because several generations of your family were born and died in it. As usual, the bedside table is full of medicine pots and bottles, while since yesterday the chest of drawers has been piled with deeds and files bearing your name, stamped in red lettering: Don Eladio Robles Sanz, Public Notary, Tamoga, waiting for you to sign them, your signature as tall and lofty as a spire. Opposite, the wardrobe mirror reflects shimmering images: that stranger standing by the bed is your son Miguel; that skinny girl running toward the door with tears in her eyes is your eldest granddaughter, and that elderly, rather plump woman who is sobbing as she kneels beside the bed is Amalia, your wife of thirty-nine years. That solemn-looking bald man, dark skinned and with angular features, who seems determined to undo the pajamas of the old man with a gray beard and fish eyes lying prostrate on the bed, and who's pressing his ear against the old man's bony chest as though he wants to hear an extraordinary secret, that serious-looking man is your friend Rey, Doctor Rey, chess-player and confirmed bachelor.

The old man is lying motionless on the bed, oblivious to everything. Through the mirror you look at that gray, dried-out skull sunk in the pillow like a stone, his bare chest cold and flat as a slab; you look at the hands resting in the folds of the turned-down sheet and think "How strange"; you move your fingers and confirm that yes, these are your hands because they obey you, you can feel them closing and opening when you want them to, and yet there they are, still and unmoving between the sheets, as distant as though they belonged to someone else, useless now because you don't need them to pick anything up, they can't grasp the air, the transparency of the air (how horrible those gnarled, hairy fingers look—like crab claws), suddenly you feel the urge to leap out of bed because this position has been uncomfortable for some time now, your back stiff and your eyes staring up at the ceiling, but you have to make sure you leave the bed without the family realizing it, they're all clustered around, you have to get out of this suffocating circle, and as you stand up none of the others even brushes against you, the air is a diaphanous wall. It takes a lot of skill to slip through this barrier of bodies; you're scared they are going to protest and prevent you from getting up, but they're too busy worshipping the bed, that heap of clothes where a decrepit body is lying. As you stretch your limbs you feel agile, walking is a new, yet very ancient, almost forgotten, pleasure, you have to think back to the earliest years of your childhood. You move cautiously, as you did then, expecting to fall over at any moment or for your bones to crack and for the pain in your joints to start again, then the choking sensation and the knot in the middle of your chest, same as before, but now you're close to the door and keep on going; your movements are gentle, as if in slow motion, as if time no longer mattered; you continue on and on, slowly advancing, but you have no idea whether it takes you seconds to reach the door or hours, years, an eternity; how to explain it, until Sir, your old setter comes in, moving his head from side to side, the twists of his fiery fur shining: his eyes have a startled look to them; it seems he's about to launch himself onto his master, but then he merely wags his tail and continues on his way.

By now you're in the hallway of the family mansion. The first novelty is the silence, a silence far more intense than there ever was here, in the sleeping house; no street noises to be heard, nor the creaking of the worm-eaten floorboards, nor the sound of your footsteps taking you to the glassed-in balcony. Through the panes you can see the square: the same square as always, except that in the middle the fountain knocked down years ago is still standing, its silver thread of water silently flowing from the slimy stone gargoyle. The eight balconies on the house opposite have been painted white, and the roof repaired; the moss has been scraped off the stonework and there is glass in the balconies again: it must be inhabited, because the main door has just opened and a carriage pulled by two horses has come to a halt outside. The driver descends from his perch, opens the carriage door, and a gentleman in a frock coat, tall boots, and a top hat gets down, accompanied by two young ladies in mourning. They all enter the house. It's hard to remember when you've seen these people before, but you're sure the taller of the two girls has green eyes, and when she is no longer young she will go to Mass every morning, and she has a missal with mother-of-pearl covers that gleam in the dark interior of the church, and she always sits near the high altar in a pew lined with red silk. The post office building has disappeared from the other corner of the square: in its place is a dilapidated shed, in whose dark doorway there is the glow of a fire; at the rear can be seen the outline of a burly man in shirtsleeves who is silently striking an anvil with a hammer. As you start to move through the house, everything becomes much closer, and you already find yourself at the far end of the corridor. You are surprised at the gaslights on the walls. You come to a halt outside the last room, the library. You hesitate for a second then decide to go in, because you can't hear any sound from the other side of the door. A slight old man with white hair and muttonchop whiskers wearing a faded blue dressing gown is seated at a writing desk with precarious-looking piles of dusty books on it. Engrossed in his reading, he occasionally dips the nib of his pen into a bronze inkwell and quickly scrawls something. At first you think he must have heard you, because he looks up and turns in your direction. You immediately recognize that little owl's head with its rimless eyelids, the astonished-looking clear eyes edged with dark circles, the short hooked nose stuck in the middle of his sallow face. It's the same old man captured in the large portrait in the drawing room, dressed elegantly in a frock coat, your great-grandfather Raimundo Robles, the family scholar, translator of Humboldt's *Cosmos* and writer on Buffon and Linnaeus, the author of an exhaustive compendium of the region's flora, and a curious monograph on Olaus Magnus. You think you spot an affectionate smile on his pursed lips, but the old man is not looking at you, he is gazing at the tiers of books filling the back wall of the room. You stand behind him and over his shoulder start to read the small, cramped letters scrawled in the margins of his voluminous tome, the flowery handwriting that used to fascinate you when you were a boy, especially the antique brown color of the ink and the shiny grains between the letters. Several plates with the remains of food stuck to them stand on a pedestal table, together with a cut glass decanter full of an amber-colored liquid. You recall the old family story praising your poor great-grandfather's passion for work, shut up in his library while his young wife grew bored in this sad, mildewed house, and only caught a glimpse of him whenever he pushed open the door just wide enough to take in the food and bottle of cold tea that he savored as though it were liquor. You respect the old man's solitude, the lonely pleasure he gets from scribbling on sheet after sheet of paper perhaps simply so that many years later a young boy will look on these hieroglyphics with wonder.

Closing the door behind you, you feel your way down the dark staircase (for a moment you're afraid you've got the wrong house) then cross the ground floor, guided by the fan of light streaming across the tiles from the doorway at the far end. The drawing room is full of people talking animatedly in silence. You are blinded by the bright light that seems to glisten from the floor, from the waxed, shiny parquet. Again you think you must be in the wrong house, because that is the only way for you to explain why all these people are dressed in such a variety of clothes from different periods. Like somebody arriving uninvited to a party, you try to mingle with the groups until you spot someone you know. A few of the guests look vaguely familiar. It takes some time for you to relate these bright, lively faces to the sepia images scattered through the old family portrait book. Near the piano, seated in a plush armchair with gilt carving, a beautiful lady aged around thirty is staring icily at the movements of the people around her. As you admire her shiny black hair falling in corkscrew ringlets down her slender neck, where a green velvet ribbon is tied, and take in her erect pose and her tight, short waist above the salmon-colored crinoline skirt, you realize this must be none other than the ravishing Edelmira, your great-grandfather's second wife. A bony sixty-year-old woman whose black shawl has slipped down her arms walks toward her and obscures your view. The doors of the drawing room that give onto the games room (closed now for more than half a century) stand wide open. In the center, a group of men are gathered around the billiard table. The same table you discovered ruined and covered in dust in the attic on one of your childhood adventures. The marble balls seem to roll for hours across the green baize; you have the feeling that time has holes in it and that you are living in several different periods at once, you can't explain it, passing from one to another just as easily as when you were a boy you used to jump from one square to another in a game of hopscotch. Your first surprise—how odd—is to find Uncle Emilio by your side, dressed as a sailor and smoking an outsize cigar; a little farther off, dozing on a sofa with his legs crossed and a newspaper unfolded across his lap like a rug, is grandfather Eladio. He is as heavy, with his waistcoat undone and his untidy hair, and as red-faced as you remember him from childhood. And that young man immaculately dressed in a white suit, with a moustache and steel-rimmed glasses, bending over the billiard table, must be none other than Claudio, your grandfather's younger brother, who emigrated to Cuba at the age of eighteen.

They look at you as if you aren't there; you're upset above all that they don't pay you the slightest attention, and this indifference becomes very painful when you go up to the man opposite you with your arms open wide, because you've recognized your father, that powerfully built man with a broad face and kindly features whom you last saw when you were seven, on a gray morning when he was brought home laid out in an old jalopy after he'd been attending a birth in a nearby village; but he (you will never forget his broad forehead or the smell of his skin) turns his back on you and walks into the drawing room rubbing his earlobe in that characteristic expression of doubt you know so well. You have to get out of here, to recover your sense of direction, to slip back into the old order, the order of time.

Now you're in the entrance hall, facing the glass door and stone staircase leading down to the garden. Beyond the steamed-up windows you can make out the rows of camellias and the chestnut tree you had chopped down a quarter of a century ago. You scarcely have time to glimpse the girl with short hair in a white skirt as she runs barelegged toward the wooden summer house half-hidden by the bougainvillea. That white shadow, cousin Nina, fades into the distance together with the memories of your first love: those desperate sleepless nights when you were fifteen, aided by a stiflingly hot summer; siestas in a hammock under the shady chestnut tree, Nina's hair against your mouth, the chamomile smell of her hair, then the rage and taste of tears when she took it into her head to get married at such a young age to that hateful stranger.

How to explain the sense of urgency, of desire, that drives you toward the sewing room, which in your childhood was nothing more than the smell of bleach and damp washing. By the window a blonde young woman is embroidering, bent over the frame; in her fingers the needle is a flash of light piercing the material. When you come in she turns her head toward the door; startled, she drops her work and runs toward you (this time there can be no doubt, she has recognized you; she is not the pitiful, delirious old woman whose death throes dragged on through an endless night, but the mother with her ample bosom who you know through memory); she hesitates a few moments, shakes her head with dismay, then steps back and makes a gesture as though to say no, but with a smile of satisfaction.

You feel an immense weight, as if your bones had filled with lead. You fall once more through the night, twist in the boundless darkness as a hot wave rises and ripples outward like an echo, and ten thousand million stars begin to shine like the lights of a distant city, and the glow is a luminous ocean, the Milky Way, and you feel once more the exhausting weight, the scurrying nervous bustle of life. Buoyed in this dark, warm bosom, you slide down, fall back until you are prone on the bed, and you hear voices that sound closer and closer, you catch words here and there . . . "adrenalin injection" . . . "cardiac arrest" . . . "he's reacted" . . . "he's coming out of it" . . . "My God, three minutes that were an eternity." You stare up in amazement at the faces bending over you around the bed, you think you've woken up from sleeping and can't understand why Amalia kisses your hands and Doctor Rey smiles and wipes his brow and your son smiles and has such a frightened look in his eyes.

VII.

DIES IRAE

As expected, when he reached the fork in the muddy track crossing the fields from the main road down to the river, he could see the house. He saw it through the slow drizzle in the uncertain light of a November dawn. The house was outside the town, surrounded by trees on a hill overlooking the plain. It was a large two-story building, the front covered in yellow tiles and with an iron balcony facing the estuary. In the distance, on the shores of the leaden sea, the lights of Tamoga were twinkling. Behind the house stood a vegetable garden surrounded by a moss-covered wall. Further on, beyond some small allotments stood the highway; beyond that, hillsides covered in dark, deep woods.

The man strode quickly toward the house, splashing carelessly through the puddles and crushing the wet grass beneath his rubber boots. He was wearing a parka with the hood pulled down over his eyes. As he walked across the flat ground in front of the house, he looked back down the way he had come. The car was out of sight. He had left it on a bend near the roadside, half-hidden behind a barrier.

He stopped in front of the entrance. The shutters on the ground floor were closed, and no chink of light shone through them. He knocked loudly several times with the giant lion's paw set in the center of the door. The blows from the doorknocker echoed like gunshots in the sleepy dawn.

After a few moments there was the sound of shutters being opened on the top floor. A window was opened halfway and a woman with white, bedraggled hair peered out.

"Who's there?" she asked.

"I need the doctor," said the man, looking up at her.

"Do you know what time it is?" the woman shouted.

She had a shrill voice, and peered down annoyed and suspicious at the dark shape standing outside the front door.

"It's very urgent. There's a man wounded nearby here."

The woman pulled her head back in. The man could hear the confused murmur of a conversation on the top floor. A few minutes later, the woman came to the window again.

"All right. He's coming," she said resignedly.

The man stood waiting in the cold drizzle. From time to time the stench of seaweed and putrefaction was wafted on the breeze. To the west, the town of Tamoga floated in a cotton-wool mist.

He heard the sound of steps slowly approaching, then a bolt grating behind the door. The woman opened it cautiously a few inches and examined him doubtfully, trying to get a good view of him. His face was still hidden in the folds of his hood.

"Come in. The doctor will be right down," said the woman, pointing inside.

The man shook each leg vigorously on the threshold to get rid of the raindrops. He bent his head as if the doorframe was too low for him, then entered the spacious, airy hallway. To his right stood a line of half a dozen chairs, all of them identical and shabby looking. At the far end was the dark recess of an open door.

"Have a seat," the woman said, offering him a chair. Her voice was friendlier now: her curiosity had gotten the better of her, and she was trying to strike up a conversation.

"Thanks," said the man, but did not sit down.

He was still standing by the half-open hall door, and had not removed his hood. In the light he seemed even heavier.

"Is it serious?" the woman asked.

She was a small woman, plump beneath her bulky clothing. Her sharp nose contrasted with her soft, placid face. There was something nunlike about it: milky white, with no sign of wrinkles, cheeks covered in a silky down. She was wearing a long brown apron with a black woolen shawl around her shoulders.

"Yes, unfortunately it is. My friend is badly wounded," the man said calmly, bending his head and staring down at the floor. "Terrible accident. The shotgun went off."

He was young and strong, and spoke very slowly, as if he had trouble pronouncing the words. His accent was not local. Although his face was still partly obscured by the shadow of the hood, the woman was certain he was not from Tamoga.

"Goodness me," she sighed. She seemed frightened.

"He's in a bad way. I think he's going to die," the man added, without raising his head. His hands were folded behind his back, and beneath his coat the cartridge belt at his waist was clearly visible.

"What happened?"

The man turned around sharply to see where this new voice had come from. A thin old man had appeared in the far doorway. He was almost bald, of average height, and not yet fully dressed. He had popped up suddenly and silently. Half of his head was completely bald; the other half was covered in a gray fuzz. Beneath his skin, the veins on his neck stood out like knotted ropes. He had a long, bony face, with sunken cheeks and a sharp, wolflike chin; his darting yellow eyes looked tiny behind his thick, wire-rimmed glasses.

Behind him was his consulting room, now lit up. Inside were a simple operating table, a cabinet full of forceps, an X-ray machine, and a screen painted with ducks flying low over water. The old man stood in the doorway, head tilted to one side, staring at the stranger. Everything about the doctor looked decrepit. Before moving forward, he blinked several times as if bewildered by the light. As he stepped into the room, however, tucking his shirttails into his trousers, his body became almost young.

The man thought the doctor was completely different from how he had imagined him.

"Doctor Lago?" he inquired, knowing beforehand what the answer would be.

The old man nodded.

"At your service," the doctor said, still unsettled.

The man stared at him for a moment before speaking. The doctor's eyes looked like two glass marbles set in the depths of his sockets.

"My friend's shotgun went off by accident. We're strangers round here," he added. "We came here to hunt. He's wounded in the stomach."

The man brought both his hands up to his belly.

"Did you say you were strangers here?" the doctor asked with a frown. His eyes were glinting now, as he surveyed the man.

"Yes."

The woman slid silently out of the room.

"Where is your friend?" asked the doctor.

"Less than a kilometer from here. I thought it was best not to move him. I left him in an abandoned hut down by the river. Near where we were hunting."

The doctor listened, still staring suspiciously at the stranger.

"They told me how to get here at the sawmills by the crossroads," the man explained.

"You should take him into town," said the doctor.

The man grimaced. He was starting to look anxious.

"All right then," said the doctor. "Let's take a look at him first."

The woman had come in again. She had a jacket, a raincoat, and a hat draped over one arm. In her free hand she was carrying a pair of shiny black galoshes. The old man finished getting dressed. His movements were precise and agile. Then he went into his consulting room and closed the door. He reappeared a few moments later with a bulky leather medical bag.

"Let's go," he said.

He waved a good-bye to his wife.

"Emilio," she called out to him. He turned back to her. "Take the umbrella with you," she said, hanging it on his arm.

The man let the doctor go first and left the house after him.

"I'll get my car out," said the doctor.

"That won't be necessary. Mine's down there," said the man. "I was afraid to drive all the way up, in case I got stuck in the mud."

As they walked down the hill, the rain came down harder. The doctor set the pace with rapid, nervous steps. When they reached the track crossing the fields down to the river, the man said:

"The car is just round the bend."

The branches of the trees lining both sides of the track arched over and made a vault.

After struggling over several meters of soaked track, they saw the car. Its snout was sticking out from the bend in the road. The doctor was surprised to see it was a Peugeot and that the license plate was French.

"You're a foreigner," he said—both an assertion and a question.

"Sort of," said the man, smiling. "I've lived in France for years."

He opened the passenger-side door, and when the doctor was installed, walked around behind the vehicle and flung himself impatiently behind the wheel. The doctor turned toward him. He blinked several times behind his glasses (a habitual mannerism, which was catching) as he studied the man's shaven head, free now from his parka's hood. The doctor looked disapprovingly and with a certain unease at the stranger's angular, dark-skinned features, and his several days' growth of beard.

"Your face looks familiar to me," said the doctor after a while. His eyes were cold and watery. He was intrigued.

"That's impossible," the man said, cutting short the conversation as he started the engine.

At first it seemed the car was going to stall, but giving out a lengthy, harsh growling sound, it lurched forward. The doctor huddled in his seat, arms folded across his chest as though he was starting to feel the cold. He sat next to the driver, staring out through the rain-swept windscreen at the blurred desolation of the fields, the dull gray of November. Every so often he looked out of the corner of his eye at the intent face of the driver, who was rocking to and fro as the car dipped and swayed in its slow advance along the muddy, bumpy track. In some places where it narrowed, branches and bushes scraped the bodywork. The man drove almost a kilometer in silence, watching for forks in the track and trying not to come out of its deep ruts.

"Nearly there," he said, slowing down.

The car entered a dense wood of pine and eucalyptus. The doctor turned to look back and caught a last glimpse of the sea. Before swiveling to face the windscreen again, he noticed the double-barreled shotgun half-hidden beneath a blanket on the back seat. Beyond the dark expanse of trees lay the marshes and the river.

The track had come to an end by now, so the car had to make its way between the pine trunks, seeking out patches of open ground, feeling its way through the low bank of fog rising from the river. The man pulled up in a clearing.

"It's here," he said, jerking his head in the direction of the sluggish river at the foot of a sandy promontory.

The doctor sat inside the car, staring at the rough pine trunks. For a moment he seemed to regret having come with the stranger. He sat in a stubborn silence that was a mirror image of the gray morning, the cold, the rainy desolation of November. Past memories soaked him like a persistent drizzle.

When he looked across again at the man, he suddenly felt immensely weary. He tried in vain to recall where and when he had seen that serious face before, with its high cheekbones and black, deep-set eyes.

The stranger grabbed the shotgun and the blanket from the back seat, got out of the car, and started to walk away. He looked back and caught sight of the doctor huddled in the front seat, his lips pursed and a lost look on his face, as if he was struggling not to show pain.

"He's an old man," the stranger thought.

"Come on," he shouted. "Come on."

Throwing the blanket over his shoulder, he took the gun and pointed the barrel toward the reed beds leading to the river.

"This way," he said, plunging through the gorse bushes and down the sandy incline.

The doctor slid down the muddy bank after him. They stepped into the reeds, which closed behind them with a rustle. The stranger walked ahead, using the gun barrel to push the stems aside.

Finally they caught sight of the abandoned cement hut (once a shelter for Civil Guardsmen who kept watch on the river) hidden among the reeds. The stranger went in first through the narrow, overgrown entrance. When the doctor followed him a few moments later, all he could make out was a dark shape in front of him. Then the harsh, high-pitched voice:

"Doctor Lago."

In the ensuing silence he could hear the stranger's uneven breathing. Taking a step to the right, away from the entrance, the doctor saw him more clearly. He was standing a few feet away, legs spread wide as he pointed the shotgun at him. The doctor stared at the stranger, a sorrowful expression on his face.

"Do you remember Celso Castillo?" the stranger growled, cocking the gun. After a tense silence in which the only sound was his own breathing, he repeated: "Do you remember?"

The doctor's lips quivered for a moment, then resumed their stubborn, tight line. He was no longer listening. He blinked at the stranger, then stared off into the dark interior of the hut. Closing his eyes, his mind went back thirty years.

In a flash of confused sensations, an instantaneous, blinding revelation, he left behind the icy November and found himself in that radiant dawn at the end of July when he and four of his friends had attacked Castillo's shop.

It was not a premeditated attack. The idea had come to them after they had spent the whole night drinking. They searched the shop, ransacking it. Kneeling on the bed in a room nearby, a young boy looked on in terror. Half-naked, the tailor's beautiful wife clutched the boy to her.

Later came the bloody chase in the hills. He no longer remembered whose idea that had been. An idea joyfully and excitedly accepted by the others, like the first day of the hunting season.

They all had shotguns, and released the tailor in the woods. "Run, Castillo," they told him. "You're going to get a chance no Red deserves."

They all, himself included, had begun to fire at the lame tailor, splitting their sides with laughter as he danced a wild, crazy dance. Castillo kept giving little leaps as he ran, and fell over bushes, legs flailing, while shots bounced around his feet and between his legs.

The chase came to an end. They all fired at point-blank range at the man clinging to the edge of the ravine.

"Do you remember? Do you remember?" the stranger's voice was a hoarse croak.

He was still pointing the shotgun at the doctor with his finger on the trigger, but he did not pull it. He was searching in the doctor's cold, yellow eyes for some sign of the terror felt by the boy he had been thirty years earlier, the terror he had always thought his father must have felt when the shotguns closed in around him.

"He's an old man," he thought, hesitating for the first time. He kept on staring at the doctor, eyes unmoving in that bony face, impassive as a death mask. He thought: "I have to shoot. I have to shoot," his mind a tumult of fury, shame, and disgust.

VIII.

ENAMORED DUST

On Ash Wednesday, when the news spread around town that Elías Rocha was on his deathbed, we all felt that, in reality, he'd already been dead a long time, since the day when infidelity and shame had made him a recluse in an old house full of shadows and memories.

That Wednesday, following his annual visit to the cemetery, the pharmacist Elías Rocha was struck down by a sudden fit of apoplexy.

He was walking back on his own as usual along the shadiest part of the Alameda when some passersby saw him suddenly halt, fling his head back, and, staring up into the sky as though searching for some sign up there, collapse to the ground a few seconds later, before anyone could run over to help him.

"It's the crazy phamacist," shouted a terrified child.

Elías Rocha was a small, painfully thin individual, with a taciturn yellowish face and skin like parchment. He always wore mourning, which contrasted with his white hair and moustache. He had bulging, pale blue eyes. Ever since his wife had run away with his only nephew, he lived alone with a maid his own age in a huge, dilapidated stone house in the center of town. On the ground floor, facing onto the Plaza del Ayuntamiento, was his pharmacy, the oldest in Tamoga.

Following the double betrayal in his family—one of the most scandalous episodes in our local history—he had withdrawn into a proud solitude that was intended to ward off both mockery and compassion. He cut himself off from all his former friends and enemies. He lived a lonely, routine existence, not bothering with anyone. He only allowed himself to be seen behind the counter in his shop, always cold and impersonal, with an inscrutable expression on his face, or at dusk in the enclosed balcony at the top of his house, sitting in a rocking chair to watch the sun go down into the Atlantic Ocean. His only contact—as superficial as it was reserved—was with Severino, his assistant at the pharmacy, his long-serving maid Encarnación, and Doctor Rey, the family doctor who had attended his mother in her dying moments.

Elías Rocha was carried unconscious to his house in a market-stall owner's van. The first vehicle to pass by, it was crammed with cages full of hens. Forty-eight hours later the pharmacist returned to the cemetery to mingle forever with the ashes of his ancestors.

Sunk in the big bed where he had come into the world seventy-something years earlier, Elías Rocha eked out his last hours without ever regaining consciousness, surrounded by the few people who, physically at least, had been close to him through twenty years of unrelenting solitude.

Early that afternoon, the parish priest came to give the last rites. Rocha looked at him without any flicker of recognition (the priest, an irascible, eloquent old man who in recent years had devoted most of his time to exorcising the devil throughout the Tamoga diocese, was of the same generation as the pharmacist—in fact, the two of them had gone to school together) and docilely allowed his body to be anointed with the holy oils.

"The flood," the dying man said with difficulty. "The flood is coming."

The priest looked at him with respectful attention, as if he had just made a prophecy.

It's possible it was Consuelo Pacheco who told the priest. That at least is what the most malicious gossip said, since Consuelo (Elías Rocha's cousin and only surviving relative in the town: a dry, snooty old spinster who had been the pharmacist's bitter enemy for years, following several arguments over the division of their maternal grandfather's estate) took advantage of the priest's visit to slip shamelessly into a house that had long been barred to her. From the start she installed herself at the dying man's bedside, with a rosary of jet beads that reached down to her feet, determined to spend his death agony muttering orations and prayers and totally ignoring the maid Encarnación's furious looks.

"This blessed scapular will restore him," said Consuelo, as though she believed it, slipping her hand underneath the pillow.

The gray light of dawn found Severino dozing exhausted in a deep mahogany armchair. Encarnación, on the other hand, stubborn and indefatigable, well used to silence and the isolation brought on by deafness, was as aware as always of every least movement from her eyrie in a corner of the bedroom. It was an enormous room, full of religious images and paintings infinitely multiplied in the mirrors lining the walls. The nervous chatter of birds singing in the garden at first light drowned out the prayers murmured by Consuelo Pacheco, half-asleep in an easy chair at the dying man's side. Soon afterwards, as Doctor Rey was about to listen again through his stethoscope, the pharmacist began muttering deliriously.

"What's he saying?" Consuelo asked anxiously.

A rattling sound made the dying man's words indistinct. His chest was rising and falling like a bellows as he wheezed his words in a weak, hollow whistle.

"He's delirious. He's saying something or other about the safe," replied Doctor Rey, pointing to a safe almost as tall as a wardrobe on the far wall of the room.

It was a black metal-bound safe with gilt moldings and inlays. An ancient, ostentatious piece, the top covered like a baroque altar with plaster saints and dried, dust-covered flowers. Most noticeable was a crucifix in the center whose base was dotted with tiny ivory skulls. In front of it a wick was constantly burning in a bowl filled with oil. These were the last vestiges of Doña Sagrario

Pacheco's pure devotion: it was said that on her wedding night she had obliged her husband to recite the complete rosary, with its fifteen mysteries and the litanies, before allowing the marriage to be consummated.

"What else is he saying?" asked Consuelo, noticing that her cousin was still moving his lips slowly.

"He's not speaking anymore," the doctor said. "He's just struggling to breathe."

Elías Rocha died at seven that morning. Making a supreme effort, in what was perhaps a final gesture of modesty, he pulled the covers up with both hands to cover his face. That was how he died, his face concealed, protecting his intimacy to the very last. His eyes were open. Death had painted a mocking grin on his bony, stern face.

"He looks happy," said Consuelo, in all seriousness. "He has the blessed look of those who are about to enter into celestial glory."

Shortly afterward, performing one last time a ceremony that had become a tradition when death entered the Rocha household, Encarnación began to turn all the mirrors in the bedroom against the wall, and stopped the hands of the grandfather clock in the main living room at exactly seven.

Against all expectations, the burial was an impressive display of widespread grief. Perhaps the sentimental wellspring of pity (everyone in Tamoga was aware of the old story, a thousand times told, of the pharmacist's unfortunate marriage) moved them to accompany en masse the man who, in his latter years, had so jealously defended his solitude.

"He's bitter," had been the usual explanation when they saw how Rocha avoided them and kept them at a distance. "He's not in his right mind," said others. The oldest among them thought back nostalgically to the days when Rocha was a cheerful, confirmed bachelor, a lover of big meals and good company at the social club. At that time, twenty years earlier, he lived with his mother and his nephew Claudio in the mansion on the square, which in earlier, more prosperous times had housed such an abundant, prolific, and private sort of family that one had to study their genealogical tree quite closely to discover who was who in the inextricable tangle of their relationships. That patriarchal world had disappeared long ago, and the Rocha family had been reduced to just three members: Doña Sagrario, her son Elías, and the grandson Claudio. And then, at the end, in the final decadence, the only one left shut away in the stone mansion on the square. Claudio was his sister's posthumous gift. She was an ugly, timid young woman by the name of Sagrario who had eloped with a traveling salesman she'd fallen head over heels in love with. They were married many kilometers from Tamoga, four months before Claudio was born. The next year she died after an abortion, and her husband wasted no time (according to him, to fulfill her dying wish) in bringing the boy to his maternal grandmother.

"At least she had the good taste not to call him Andrelino," (Andrelino was the name of the commercial traveler) was Doña Sagrario's sour comment when she first saw her grandson. However, her disgust soon evaporated, and for a few years she even began to bend a little, making the unlikely transformation into a sweet, dot-ing grandmother.

When he brought his son to Tamoga, the salesman promised he would return.

"I'll send you my address once I know where I'm based," he said. That was the last they heard of him.

This meant that Doña Sagrario and her son were left with the responsibility of bringing up the boy. As he grew, he began to look more and more like his mother: from her he inherited the same shyness, the same sad, moist eyes, the same languid gestures, and the same fatal propensity—as was later demon-strated—for running away.

Elías Rocha paid for his nephew's studies, encouraging him to become a pharmacist so as to continue the family tradition. A month after Claudio had graduated, Doña Sagrario died at the age of eighty-five. Lucid until the last minute, she confronted death with the proud disdain and courage that had characterized her entire life. Possibly she had been waiting for this very moment to die, because she had been gravely ill for a year but had assured Doctor Rey she would not leave this world until she was sure there was a new pharmacist in the family.

"I'm coming, Claudio. You won't have to wait any longer," it's said that Doña Sagrario Pacheco sighed in the minutes before she breathed her last. (Claudio, her husband, had left her a widow in her prime, fifty years earlier.)

Before the year was out, to everyone's amazement, Elías Rocha got married. Somebody even claimed that on her deathbed Doña

Sagrario had made her son promise he would marry once she was gone.

"Find yourself a clean, pious woman," they say Doña Sagrario told him. In that order. This at least fits her eccentric character.

Doña Sagrario, who would never have put up with a rival while she was alive (she strongly discouraged her son whenever he seemed about to commit the slightest indiscretion) possibly thought it was a good idea if after her death a woman was on hand to take over running the house and looking after the pharmacist in the difficult years of encroaching old age. If the report is true (there are reasons to believe that Doña Sagrario, on the contrary, would revolve in her grave if she knew a stranger was going to take her place in the old house on the square, where she had reigned supreme for more than sixty years), there's no doubt that Elías Rocha took little time to fulfill her wishes.

Nobody knows how Rocha and Magana met. So many outlandish and contradictory rumors were spread that even today it's a mystery as to where the girl who so captivated the fifty-year-old bachelor sprang from. All we know is that Elías Rocha met her in a town on the coast on the other side of the border. It's also quite likely that the rumor placing her as a waitress in a tearoom has some truth to it.

In any case, the fact is that one fine day they turned up in the town married, after Elías Rocha had made a lightning six-day trip. In those days, the pharmacist used to cross the border quite often (the reason for these trips was a mystery, although there were rumors that it was to speculate in gold and currency). He must have met the girl on one of these journeys and fell instantly and madly in love with her, because all of a sudden he returned to Tamoga married, happy, and even looking rejuvenated.

This was such a surprise that it took the town a while to associate the unassuming, middle-aged pharmacist with the fresh-faced stranger who was his wife, though young enough to be his daughter. Her name was Magana (that was all we knew about her) and she didn't seem to be much older than twenty. She was slender, attractive, and wore her jet-black hair cut short like a boy. Her body was lean but flexible, with gentle, gracious curves, the body of a splendid adolescent who has only just grown to maturity. Her vaguely childish air was somehow disturbing.

The inhabitants of Tamoga were able to get a good view of her for the first time at the end of twelve o'clock Mass on the Sunday following her arrival in town. To most of them it was a scandal to see such a striking young woman on the arm of the middle-aged pharmacist. Even during Mass, some of the old biddies had begun to whisper their harsh verdicts on her, completely ignoring the priest's stirring sermon as he raged in his pulpit, trying to convince the congregation that the devil was forever on the prowl in Tamoga.

"She's only a slip of a girl," they muttered. "Heaven knows where he kidnapped her."

Outside the church after Mass, the women looked her up and down quite openly, then decreed that her dress was too short, was provocative and vulgar. The men on the other hand gawped at her lasciviously, making risqué remarks.

From that Sunday midday on, Magana flaunted her dazzling beauty all around the town.

Since, till now, Claudio had been regarded as Elías Rocha's heir, many in the town predicted it wouldn't be long before hostilities began between the nephew and his brand-new young aunt: hidden and secretive at first, these would surely burst out into the open and become public before too long.

They were disappointed however, because not only did Claudio seem pleased with his uncle's unexpected marriage, he became Magana's comrade, guide, and faithful companion.

They often went on excursions; in summer they went down to the beach every morning; they played together in the tennis tournament organized by the local club; and they never missed any of the dances the social club put on. Elías Rocha sometimes accompanied them, but never wanted to dance: to him it was a waste of time, a boring form of exercise.

As was to be expected, the town rumors changed in tone. The gossip—which spread like lightning almost as soon as it started in the barbershops and back rooms, among groups of people with nothing better to do, sewing circles, social gatherings—turned now to the rivalry between uncle and nephew, family disputes, even a major scandal that might enliven their small-town boredom for months. All this muttering was based not so much on anything concrete as on the resentment felt by all those who thought Elías Rocha was too old for such a young woman, and that she was far too alluring. Despite the impatience of these prophets of doom, the Rocha family continued on its way unperturbed. There was perfect family harmony, and the marriage, at least on the surface, seemed to be as happy as it had been at the beginning.

On afternoons when it wasn't raining, Claudio and Magana went out for bicycle rides. They would pedal furiously through the town out along the coast road, pursued by their neighbors' curious, often ill-intentioned stares.

They almost always followed the same route, and were so punctual that some of the members of the social club who were dozing off by the big window overlooking the highway used to instinctively consult their watches to see if it was really four o'clock already.

"There go the turtledoves," they would say with a yawn.

The sight of a pair of perfect tanned bare legs that seemed to go on forever was a pleasant daily distraction on those summer afternoons.

When September and its drowsy evenings arrived, the two would walk down to the port. Sometimes they would go into a fishermen's bar, spend a long time in animated conversation, then prolong their outing by carrying on to Puerto Angra. There they would stand by the customs house watching the maneuvers of the ferry boats that crossed the estuary, and the blood-red sunsets that stretched from the border right out to the horizon at sea.

Their happy, unconcerned appearance, their casual indifference to what anyone thought, was a serious challenge to the blinkered, jealous world of Tamoga.

Then all of a sudden they were no longer seen together.

All the rumors must have finally reached their ears, people said.

From then on, Magana only appeared in public with her husband, while Claudio spent many more hours than before in the pharmacy, attending to the customers. The assistant, Severino, was the first to be surprised at the zeal and enthusiasm that Don Elías's nephew showed for his work. He was even more astonished when Claudio himself offered to take his place when the pharmacy was open late.

It also surprised many people in Tamoga when Elías Rocha suddenly stopped attending his usual social evenings at the club, and although he remained as polite as ever, he began to distance himself from his friends and to become more and more reserved. He was obviously shunning all outside contact.

Magana was still the carefree young woman who had arrived in town a year earlier, but there was something different about her, a forced expression which suggested she was tired, or fighting something: the sign of internal tension. Many people concluded that the gossip had created a sense of shame, indignation, or even suspicion among the members of the Rocha family, and had poisoned their relationships. Others were inclined to believe that Magana was suffering the pangs of a forbidden love (something that was not entirely improbable).

Then for several months the whole town became fascinated by the regular visits Magana made to Doctor Rey's office. "She's sick," some people said. "She's expecting a child," the more experienced observed. And they were right. Magana now proudly displayed the beginnings of a bulge, which she accentuated by wearing tight, flimsy garments.

To the oldest Tamogans, who had known three generations of the Rocha family and remembered how calculating and rapacious they were ("An endemic plague about to be eradicated from Tamoga," Doctor Lago was to say years later; his own family had had political skirmishes with them since time immemorial)—it was obvious that the pharmacist had planned the child before the marriage. So it had been no crazy autumnal passion—the townspeople thought without a scrap of logic—but a deliberate move, coldly calculated like a business affair, with the aim of continuing the Rocha line. "That's why he chose such a young filly," they told each other. Despite this, some wagging tongues soon decided it was the nephew's handiwork.

So the whole town closely followed Magana's pregnancy. As usual, the most knowledgeable women exchanged opinions on the exact date of birth, the possible complications, and the gender of the future Rocha—although most of them predicted it would be a boy. The men meanwhile were more interested in knowing whom the child would look like.

"Whatever happens, there'll be a family likeness," joked one wit.

It was two or three months before the inhabitants of Tamoga were to have their curiosity satisfied (as they could tell from Magana's swelling belly)—when the scandal that shook the entire town occurred, one that was only relived at the moment of the pharmacist's death.

One rainy, tedious afternoon at the end of autumn, Bravo, the manager of the telegraph office, looked out of his office window and saw Rocha striding across the rain-swept, deserted Plaza

Nueva, then go into the police station after hesitating a few moments under the painted sign on the door. According to Bravo, the pharmacist was staggering like a drunkard (a detail perhaps invented by the telegraphist to impress his audience), and his clothes were streaming wet.

As always he was dressed in black, and he was not wearing a raincoat or carrying an umbrella—the telegraphist said. "What most astonished me was how disheveled he looked."

No one knows exactly what was said that afternoon between Elías Rocha and the police chief. Out of the mass of gossip and reckless speculation that spread through the town, all that's known for certain is that Rocha reported the disappearance of his wife and his nephew Claudio. It also transpired that the pharmacist waited three whole days (perhaps hoping the couple would repent and return) before making his report. So by the time the inhabitants of Tamoga got wind of it, the fugitives were already three days away from Tamoga.

Although there were no eyewitnesses (the interview between the jilted husband and the inspector took place privately, in the latter's office) those who claimed to be in the know said it wasn't his wife's disappearance that Rocha had reported, but that of the valuable family jewels that once belonged to Doña Sagrario Pachecho, his mother, which the fleeing lovers must have stolen. The story of the theft was never confirmed, although no one ever took it upon themselves to deny it either. The real facts were concealed in the statements held by the court and the police. Despite the police's discretion, what's known for sure is that Elías

Rocha gave the inspector a note written in a ceremonious, high-flown style, and signed by the two lovers. In it they informed the pharmacist of their decision to elope, and in an insincere postscript asked for his forgiveness.

The pharmacist's visit to the inspector can be reconstructed easily enough: Rocha, still stunned by what had happened, would have told the chief about it in a hoarse whisper. The monumental, phlegmatic inspector (Cardona is almost two meters tall and weighs more than a hundred kilos) would have invited him to sit down, but Rocha doubtlessly ignored the invitation and remained standing, telling the story in an increasingly rapid torrent. The inspector would have listened to him imperturbably, shielded behind his desk and smoking nonstop.

"Go on, go on," the inspector would have urged him, whenever it looked as if Rocha was losing the thread.

Wreathed in cigarette smoke, from time to time the inspector would clear his throat and tactfully interrupt the confused tale to ask the pharmacist to clarify a detail or repeat something that had come out in a jumble. Rocha would begin again or gabble something vague if he couldn't think of a proper reply. Finally, it's likely that Cardona accompanied the pharmacist to the door, patting him on the back in a friendly way and speaking quietly to him as if in condolence, leaning over him with a protective gesture like a master instructing a disciple (the difference in size between the pharmacist's slight frame and the inspector's massive bulk would have been comical), and then probably bid him good-bye with an effusive, lengthy handshake.

"Well, we'll see . . ." was the inspector's habitually evasive farewell.

As a result of these unheard-of events, an endless number of rumors began to circulate, spreading the wildest, most outlandish stories about the parties involved. It was said that before she met the chemist, Magana had been a scantily clad dancer in a funfair sideshow. Somebody swore Claudio and Magana often met at a beach hotel on the other side of the border, and that it was the nephew who planned the meeting between her and his uncle. We never found out if these rumors, which were impossible to verify, had any grain of truth to them, or were as nonsensical as all the others in Tamoga.

Some days after their interview, Inspector Cardona went down to Puerto Angra. From there he took the postal launch that crosses the border twice a day. He visited a hotel on the beach, an ugly, square cement building that had a terrace and balconies facing the sea. He poked around, tried to investigate, and drilled the owner—a potbellied Portuguese with a high-pitched voice—with questions to which the latter gave only evasive replies. The owner remembered the two young people but could not be certain about the dates they had stayed at the hotel—which had, in any case, always been for a few hours only. They had never spent the night there. Cardona retraced their steps, as outlined by the hotel owner. A kind of sentimental journey. It's easy to imagine the slow-moving Cardona struggling up and down the sand dunes, the tails of his raincoat flapping and his hair tousled by the wind, his bulky figure standing out against the gray sky and foaming sea. He walked along the deserted beach with only sea birds for company. He visited other coastal establishments. In some of them they had a vague recollection of the pair. Behind the counter of a corner store bar near the estuary, an old woman was more forthcoming.

"Yes, I saw the couple some evenings," she said. "They would walk along the beach arm-in-arm. But they were soon hidden by the dunes. Look out of this window, Inspector. That's where I saw them from."

Cardona went back to the hotel, talked to the waiters, asked questions until he grew tired of it. By the time he returned to Tamoga, he knew a lot about the two young people's amorous habits, but had no definite lead apart from a few isolated, worthless facts which, like his footprints in the sand, led nowhere.

Time went by, and nobody was any the wiser as to the whereabouts of the pharmacist's wife and nephew. Perhaps Magana had no family, or had no contact with them, because no one ever came looking for her or asked what might have become of her.

One version had it that the lovers had crossed the border in secret. According to another, they had fled to another part of the country; a third suggestion was that they had put the sea between them and the husband. Pure guesswork. Every year some traveler or emigrant returning to the town swore they had seen them in a far-off place. They obviously had a genius for being ubiquitous, because they were spotted at more or less the same time in Lisbon, Buenos Aires, Recife, Cumaná, and God knows where else. Later on, these versions were modified, the rumors embellished. Everyone knows that the popular imagination is capable of endless variety.

And so, ever since the couple vanished, no one was able to say with any certainty where they were. From the moment of their ill-omened flight, Elías Rocha was finished (not only because of his wife's betrayal, but even more that of his nephew, whom he had brought up as a son). He aged astonishingly quickly, and shut himself into a silence and solitude that over the next twenty years became his defining characteristics.

At first, although of course there was absolutely no basis for it, it was said in Tamoga that he had lost his reason. Curious but terrified school kids would creep up to the door of the pharmacy then race off as soon as they caught sight of him behind the counter.

"Here comes the mad pharmacist," they would shriek with excitement.

People stared somewhat apprehensively at the closed shutters of the three-story house where the pharmacist lived his reclusive life. For a while, many of his former customers refused to buy anything at the Rocha pharmacy. Little by little, however, time allayed their suspicions, and in his later years the figure of the harmless, lonely old man only aroused curiosity and a compassionate, slightly mocking tolerance among the townsfolk.

Following his burial (the entire town thought it was their pious duty to accompany the body from the mansion to the cemetery), there was much speculation about the possible fate of his fortune.

In spite of the rain falling endlessly that afternoon, it was impossible to imagine a better turnout. The coffin was in a hearse pulled by two bedraggled old nags with black plumes on their heads; they slipped at every step on the wet cobbles of the streets of Tamoga.

Elías Rocha's former friends had claimed the right to carry the coffin on their shoulders out of the house and to the hearse waiting in the square. As they came down the steps, they almost dropped it when they found the weight was too much for them, while the crowd of people filling the street or peering from balconies and windows had to witness the depressing sight of six decrepit old men struggling to control this magnificent coffin with its bronze handles, covered in two huge, impressive wreaths.

The procession fell in behind the hearse and made its way in perfect order along the half-flooded main streets of Tamoga and out to the cemetery.

Even before the body was in the ground, many people were speculating that Elías Rocha had amassed a considerable fortune through scrimping and saving. He was known to be a miser. In addition, his family fortune (one of the largest in Tamoga) consisted of several houses, two large plots of land, which with the years had become properties in the center of town, and some of the best woodlands in the hills, with stands of pine and eucalyptus.

Although nobody knew whether Rocha had made a will, it was generally assumed he had left all he had to his maid Encarnación (his old servant—a tiny woman who with the years had become so wrinkled and stooped that nobody could have imagined that fifty years earlier this scrawny bag of cracking bones had been a resplendent beauty who had claimed the hearts of many men—who had been employed by the Rocha family for nearly sixty years) and to his faithful assistant Severino, who had been working in the pharmacy for more than thirty years.

The day after the funeral, following a request by Consuelo Pacheco, who as the pharmacist's cousin and only relative considered herself his rightful heir, a commission of prominent people from the town got together to go through all the dead man's papers, draw up an inventory of his possessions, and search for the will that everyone talked about as though they knew for a fact that it existed.

That memorable day the members of this commission made their way to the old Rocha house. There was the mayor, the parish priest, the police chief, the magistrate, the public notary, Doctor Rey, and two of Tamoga's leading businessmen. They banged on the heavy bronze front door knocker for almost ten minutes.

"The maid is deaf," Doctor Rey explained.

Old Encarnación finally came slowly down the stairs, muttering incomprehensible words under her breath. She was dressed in black from head to toe, with a few strands of ash-gray hair fallen over her eyes. Confused and annoyed, she gazed suspiciously at the men as she opened a front door that none of them, apart from the priest and Doctor Rey, had ever crossed. They fumbled their way across the large, gloomy hallway that was filled with the dense soporific smell of drugs, unguents, and medicinal herbs that must be wafting through from the pharmacy next door.

Once their eyes grew accustomed to the gloom, they could make out another room off the hall, which had at one time been a stable. In it were a carriage lacking its front wheels, and a Ford sedan from 1915, covered in dust and cobwebs. (The battered Ford, which had traveled all the roads in the region, had been the indispensable ally of the amorous adventures of Américo Pacheco, the pharmacist's maternal uncle. A legendary rake in our local history, it was said he died one night aged over seventy when his heart gave out as he was trying to scale a wall that proved too high for him).

"Be careful with the handrail," Doctor Rey warned the others. "It's rotten."

Encarnación led the visitors up the stairs and along the top floor corridor, which was lit by a grimy skylight. She halted outside a door locked with an enormous padlock.

"The master's study," she said, pulling a jangling set of keys out from her apron.

They went into another gloomy room, lined with ocher and gold wallpaper spotted with patches of damp. There was a broad table, a chair covered in cracked leather, a glass-fronted cabinet, half a dozen chairs, and a marble-topped console table crammed with ornaments: knickknacks, a clock inside a bell jar, and two big vases full of red cloth roses.

The air in the room was musty. On the far wall to the right of the only window hung a darkened oil painting depicting an old man with a stern scowl on his face (this was Dalmiro Rocha, the grandfather of the pharmacist) dressed in a frock coat.

The table was piled high with yellowing papers, warped folders, bits of string, pens, and balls of sealing wax, as well as old newspapers and calendars. On one corner of the table two frames faced each other. One hand-tinted photograph showed the wife, Magana (with her hair cut very short and in a low-cut pink sleeveless dress), smiling for eternity. In the other, smaller photograph a skinny little boy could be seen, a nervous expression on his face and an evasive, sad look in his eyes. He was dressed for first communion. A dedication was written across the bottom of the portrait in big letters: "To my beloved uncle, in memory of the happiest day of my life, with all love from his nephew Claudio."

It took them more than two hours of careful inspection to find out that the table only contained unimportant documents: bills, business letters, prescriptions, catalogues, and old account books containing a scrupulous register, over more than a century, of the smallest transactions: the income and rents from the family properties as well as the debit and credit accounts for the Rocha pharmacy since it opened its doors. The cabinet contained nothing more than religious tomes: prayer books, missals, hagiographies of saints and martyrs, a Bible with moth-eaten covers, its first pages scribbled over with names, dates, and little crosses traced in faded brown ink. Finally, in one of the table drawers, they found a thick bundle of shares in a Portuguese maritime company and a porcelain pot full of antique gold coins. That was all. They were on the point of giving up their search when Consuelo Pacheco came into the room.

"There's a safe in my cousin's bedroom," she said. "It's locked."

A futile search followed for the strongbox's combination. Neither Severino nor Encarnación had any idea what it was.

They had to send for Mosquera the locksmith.

With great reluctance, Encarnación opened the vast bedroom for them. She stared at Mosquera and his assistant weighed down with blowtorches, crowbars, wrenches, and chisels, as if they were two burglars about to empty the house.

As Mosquera was lighting the blowtorch, he was startled to hear her shout at him:

"Savages!"

Encarnación was protesting desperately at the damage they were going to cause. It took all Doctor Rey's patience to convince her it was absolutely necessary to force the safe open. Somewhat mollified by the doctor's words, and with the promise that the locksmiths were not going to set fire to the house or get the bedroom dirty, Encarnación left the room, still muttering insults. She took up her post in the next room, from where she could keep a close watch on the comings and goings of the intruders.

Even though the two men worked hard all the rest of the day, it wasn't until around eleven o'clock the next morning that they managed to force open the complicated lock on the strongbox.

"Finished," Mosquera announced, puffing out his cheeks with satisfaction.

Severino ran to tell the magistrate, who at that moment was in the courtroom. Minutes later they were all gathered around the imposing, solid box.

The light filtering in through the purple curtains gave a reddish glow to the headboard of the bed where Elías Rocha had died.

Grasping the big gilt eyebolt in the center of the safe front, Mosquera glanced inquiringly over at the magistrate. When the latter nodded, after looking in turn at the priest and the inspector, Mosquera pulled on the bolt, and the heavy door swung open with a loud grating noise. A bitter, pungent smell invaded the room.

Consuelo Pacheco cried out and staggered backwards, pointing to the dark shadows inside the half-open safe.

Curled up like twin fetuses in a gigantic, dusty womb, two mummies decked out in the finest jewels (necklaces, bracelets, and bangles gleamed, sunk in the shriveled flesh) stared at the visitors. From the ghastly intensity of fleshless, empty eye sockets, Magana and Claudio stared out from the depths of their metal tomb.

IX.

THE RIVER WITHOUT BANKS

On the night in October following his sixtieth birthday, José-Augusto Iglesias woke up soaked in sweat in the middle of a sad, oppressive dream.

"Cecilia, Cecilia," he called out softly, still half-asleep, feeling for the far side of the pillow. Seconds after pronouncing his wife's name, he was painfully aware yet again of the hollow in their bed, the space forever empty.

His wife had died four months earlier, but force of habit led him to still call to her when he awoke from a nightmare, as he had done when she shared the covers. For a moment he always seemed to forget she was buried beneath the ground and he was alone in the solitude of their bed.

He was tall and thin, with gray hair and a face more wrinkled than his years suggested. His bony forehead was furrowed with thick veins, his cheeks sunken. He had big, bright green eyes that seemed to be perpetually wide with astonishment.

He sat up in bed, yawned, and rubbed the sleep from his eyes with his knuckles. Pushing the mosquito net open, he jumped out of bed. He could see from the dark windows that it was still several hours before dawn. The constant drumming of raindrops on the tin roof had been drilling into his brain for a week now. He lay down again and felt for the tobacco and matches on the bedside table, careful not to knock over his glasses or the water jug. As he smoked in the darkness, blowing smoke at his glowing cigarette tip, he tried to remember all the details of his dream. He recalled the ridiculous succession of events, and also recalled with astonishment that he had dreamed exactly the same thing a few months earlier, just before his wife had died. Then as now, he had dreamed of a large, sad town built between the sea and a river estuary.

This was his dream. He was walking along a deserted street, lined on both sides by big stone houses. Their doors and windows were shut. In the distance he spied a ragged old man with white hair and beard, limping toward him leaning on a stick. When the old man came within earshot, he decided to ask him the name of the town. The old man must have read his mind, because before José-Augusto could even move his lips, he pointed his stick at the houses clustered at the foot of a hill and said, "Tamoga!"

José-Augusto Iglesias went on walking until he realized the street ended in a cemetery. Soon after he had gone inside, the old man appeared again, although this time his face was covered in a bird mask. He was standing outside a ruined vault, signaling for him to come nearer. When José-Augusto was close, he looked in the niches for the dates and names engraved there. The old man watched as José-Augusto began to clean the mud off the plaques. When he raised his head, still out of breath, the old man said: "They will sleep here forever." At this, the sky grew dark and a cloud of dust swirled around him. The old man collapsed in a heap of ashes and more dust; vaults, crosses, statues, and cypresses too all fell into dust. José Antonio opened his mouth, but could not say a word because he was enveloped in a thick shroud of ashes: his mouth, eyes, nostrils were all filled with earth and he was slowly suffocating.

At that moment he woke up, agonized and bewildered. His tongue was rough, his breathing uneven, as though the earth and the suffocation of his dream were real.

He spent the rest of the night in the grip of insomnia. Disturbed by the nightmare, overcome by nostalgia, he went over and over in his mind what he had done with his life.

"The results are bitter and discouraging," he told himself, still stretched out on the bed.

Since his wife's death, he had lived alone in the house, a one-story building that contained his bedroom, office, and storeroom. His business as a pharmaceutical representative meant he was often away visiting the other towns in the region. Despite the fact that he was beginning to feel old and tired, he preferred the discomfort of travel to the torture of staying in an empty, silent house, where every corner was steeped in memories of his wife.

Many nights he roamed around it, expecting at any moment to bump into her. He couldn't help but feel that if she only knew how badly her husband was missing her, she would come back and never leave him again.

One night, perhaps even sadder and more desolate than the ones that had gone before, he sat up until dawn drinking a harsh, strong rum that burned his throat, in the hope it would drive the image of his wife out of his mind. When he stumbled into the sewing room he almost cried out. A dark mass lay in the rocking chair where his wife used to sit. He gave a strangled cry of dismay when he realized it was nothing more than a bundle of laundry the housekeeper had left there. He had never felt so useless, desolate, and alone as he did then, standing in the suffocating darkness, his body wracked by drunken sobs. He suddenly lost his conviction that the dead could reawaken simply thanks to the nostalgia, despair, and sheer strength of desire felt by those still alive. In his sad but lucid drunkenness he understood that he and his wife were separated forever, because it is impossible to go back in time, the past cannot be repeated, and no magic spell or wish, however sincere, would bring her back from the shadows.

He had been in the country ten years when he met Cecilia. She was a maid at the cheap hotel where he was staying. One night, several months after meeting her, he succeeded in getting her into his room. They continued in the same way for almost a year, meeting in secret and running the risk the hotel would find out. "If you can convince me, I'll marry you," he had promised her. And José-Augusto had never repented his decision. They had lived in perfect harmony through thirty years of marriage. Then she had died, when he had become completely accustomed to her silent presence

("You're like an Indian woman," he used to say when he saw her gliding noiselessly barefoot around the house), just when he was going to need her the most, as old age beckoned.

The idea of returning to the town where he was born, if only for a brief visit, came to him during those monotonous, forlorn days and sleepless nights that so exasperated him.

He had managed to put aside some savings. Until his wife's death, he had been a contented emigrant, with a flourishing business and a good reputation that spread from Barranquilla to Santa Marta on Colombia's Caribbean coast. He had no children or relatives. He had been so caught up in his work that he had made few friends. Now the solitude was so unbearable that he sometimes found he was muttering to himself or holding animated conversations with no one.

"I'm going off my head," he told himself calmly. "My brain's turning to mush."

He was born in a town called Tamoga, on the far side of the Atlantic. Since he left, before his twentieth birthday, he had never missed the place. He hadn't left because he was going hungry, but because he needed to escape a stifling atmosphere that seemed to him frustrating and tedious—only to discover later on that life can be equally tedious, boring, and stifling on the other side of the ocean. His parents and his only brother had died many years before. All he had left in the town were a few distant relatives he barely knew.

He returned to Tamoga at the end of December. He had been away for so long he took it for granted nobody in the town would recognize him. He traveled by ship as far as Lisbon. One calm, starry night in midocean, the cosmic silence and boundless solitude enveloping the ship made him realize he wouldn't be able to overcome his tremendous sense of impatience until he once more saw the coast where he had spent his childhood.

He made the rest of the journey to Tamoga in a battered old Buick sold to him by a Brazilian who was going back to his own country. The car was too old, and had been patched up with spare parts from a variety of different vehicles, but he bought it because it was cheap and because the Brazilian reminded him of one of his few friends in Barranquilla: a fellow countryman with a serious, intelligent-looking face who ran a pharmacy in Paseo Colón. So he bought it on a nostalgic impulse.

Half an hour after crossing the border, he saw the town from the top of a low rise.

It had been so long, and the town was so blurred and distant as it floated between mist and water, that it didn't look real. The wide, dark river flowed down past the left-hand side of the highway to lose itself in the sea on the horizon. Some long-haired ponies were grazing in the mud of the river marshes.

Shortly afterward, in the early hours of the morning, he began his slow entry into Tamoga. He saw the Alameda with its lines of plane trees, limes, and rustling palms, and the iron bandstand at its center. He saw the first houses, just the same as they had been in his childhood: some of them made of stone, others with their fronts covered in tiles, set in gardens surrounded by railings.

He parked the car in the middle of town, got out, and stood staring at the house where he was born. It was a big old stone building, with carved wooden eaves and two enclosed balconies on the front. José-Augusto studied it through the rain until he suddenly realized he was shivering with cold. "Everything is the same as it used to be," he thought.

Getting back into his car, he decided to visit the cemetery despite the pouring rain and cold. "First I go straight on, then I have to turn left and continue along the coast road," he told himself, starting up the Buick.

He soon left the last houses of Tamoga behind and then drove rapidly along the highway that twisted and turned through the pine and eucalyptus woods. He caught glimpses of the gray, sluggish river through gaps in the trees. The wiper smeared the windscreen, then offered a clear view of the flat stretch of land in front of him. As he went around a bend near the cemetery he was struck by the sight of a stone cross by the roadside. A few yards further on, he could see the cemetery's white walls, the bare hills, and the gray waters of the river broadening out to the sea.

A small, hunchbacked man protected from the rain by an umbrella was opening the cemetery gate.

"That cross over there . . ." asked José-Augusto, intrigued.

He had to repeat his question.

"Ah, that marks the spot of an accident," the man spluttered through a coughing fit. "A stranger who drove round the bend like a madman and was flattened by a truck."

José-Augusto found his way through the maze of crosses and tombs straight to the family vault. He had not been back there since he accompanied his mother to the cemetery a few months before he left Tamoga.

The headstones shone, washed clean by the rain. With a lump in his throat he read the names and dates. As he deciphered the inscriptions, he was overwhelmed by so many memories that in the end he wasn't sure whether he was actually reading them or summoning them up through sheer nostalgia.

First of all he read his mother's name, and the two dates marking her passage through this world. Then in the niche below hers he saw his father's epitaph, the first of a long list dotted with dates and crosses. Astonished, he read the last of them. Unable to believe his eyes, he studied it carefully a second time. "Perhaps it's a mistake," he told himself. He looked around for the way out. He shouted for the man who had opened the gate for him. Nobody came. He pushed the gate open and ran to his car. "I'm in the dream," he thought. "I'm soaked to the skin, and I'm freezing cold," he said, trying to rationalize his feelings.

The car sped along the flooded highway. The countryside was a dark stain, a shadow under water. The torrential rain fell like a curtain in front of his eyes. As he went around the sharp bend where he had seen the stone cross, José-Augusto exclaimed in surprise: "I could have sworn the cross was here."

He had no time to say anything more. At that instant a truck coming in the opposite direction skidded on the bend and crashed into him at full speed.

"For we are but of yesterday, and know nothing,
because our days upon earth are a shadow."

JOB 8, 9

JULIÁN RÍOS is Spain's foremost postmodernist writer. After co-authoring two books with Octavio Paz, Ríos went on to write numerous works of fiction and nonfiction, including *Larva, Poundemonium, Loves That Bind,* and *Monstruary,* all of which have been published in English translation. He lives in Paris.

NICK CAISTOR is a translator, editor, and author. He has written a biography of Octavio Paz and has translated works by José Saramago, Juan Marsé, and Eduardo Mendoza, among others.

SELECTED DALKEY ARCHIVE PAPERBACKS

FOR A FULL LIST OF PUBLICATIONS, VISIT:
www.dalkeyarchive.com

SELECTED DALKEY ARCHIVE PAPERBACKS

CARLOS FUENTES, *Christopher Unborn.*
  Distant Relations.
  Terra Nostra.
  Where the Air Is Clear.
JANICE GALLOWAY, *Foreign Parts.*
  The Trick Is to Keep Breathing.
WILLIAM H. GASS, *Cartesian Sonata*
  and Other Novellas.
  Finding a Form.
  A Temple of Texts.
  The Tunnel.
  Willie Masters' Lonesome Wife.
GÉRARD GAVARRY, *Hoppla! 1 2 3.*
  Making a Novel.
ETIENNE GILSON,
  The Arts of the Beautiful.
  Forms and Substances in the Arts.
C. S. GISCOMBE, *Giscome Road.*
  Here.
  Prairie Style.
DOUGLAS GLOVER, *Bad News of the Heart.*
  The Enamoured Knight.
WITOLD GOMBROWICZ,
  A Kind of Testament.
KAREN ELIZABETH GORDON,
  The Red Shoes.
GEORGI GOSPODINOV, *Natural Novel.*
JUAN GOYTISOLO, *Count Julian.*
  Exiled from Almost Everywhere.
  Juan the Landless.
  Makbara.
  Marks of Identity.
PATRICK GRAINVILLE, *The Cave of Heaven.*
HENRY GREEN, *Back.*
  Blindness.
  Concluding.
  Doting.
  Nothing.
JIŘÍ GRUŠA, *The Questionnaire.*
GABRIEL GUDDING,
  Rhode Island Notebook.
MELA HARTWIG, *Am I a Redundant*
  Human Being?
JOHN HAWKES, *The Passion Artist.*
  Whistlejacket.
ALEKSANDAR HEMON, ED.,
  Best European Fiction.
AIDAN HIGGINS, *A Bestiary.*
  Balcony of Europe.
  Bornholm Night-Ferry.
  Darkling Plain: Texts for the Air.
  Flotsam and Jetsam.
  Langrishe, Go Down.
  Scenes from a Receding Past.
  Windy Arbours.
KEIZO HINO, *Isle of Dreams.*
KAZUSHI HOSAKA, *Plainsong.*
ALDOUS HUXLEY, *Antic Hay.*
  Crome Yellow.
  Point Counter Point.
  Those Barren Leaves.
  Time Must Have a Stop.
NAOYUKI II, *The Shadow of a Blue Cat.*
MIKHAIL IOSSEL AND JEFF PARKER, EDS.,
  Amerika: Russian Writers View the
  United States.
GERT JONKE, *The Distant Sound.*
  Geometric Regional Novel.
  Homage to Czerny.
  The System of Vienna.

JACQUES JOUET, *Mountain R.*
  Savage.
  Upstaged.
CHARLES JULIET, *Conversations with*
  Samuel Beckett and Bram van
  Velde.
MIEKO KANAI, *The Word Book.*
YORAM KANIUK, *Life on Sandpaper.*
HUGH KENNER, *The Counterfeiters.*
  Flaubert, Joyce and Beckett:
  The Stoic Comedians.
  Joyce's Voices.
DANILO KIŠ, *Garden, Ashes.*
  A Tomb for Boris Davidovich.
ANITA KONKKA, *A Fool's Paradise.*
GEORGE KONRÁD, *The City Builder.*
TADEUSZ KONWICKI, *A Minor Apocalypse.*
  The Polish Complex.
MENIS KOUMANDAREAS, *Koula.*
ELAINE KRAF, *The Princess of 72nd Street.*
JIM KRUSOE, *Iceland.*
EWA KURYLUK, *Century 21.*
EMILIO LASCANO TEGUI, *On Elegance*
  While Sleeping.
ERIC LAURRENT, *Do Not Touch.*
HERVÉ LE TELLIER, *The Sextine Chapel.*
  A Thousand Pearls (for a Thousand
  Pennies)
VIOLETTE LEDUC, *La Bâtarde.*
EDOUARD LEVÉ, *Suicide.*
SUZANNE JILL LEVINE, *The Subversive*
  Scribe: Translating Latin
  American Fiction.
DEBORAH LEVY, *Billy and Girl.*
  Pillow Talk in Europe and Other
  Places.
JOSÉ LEZAMA LIMA, *Paradiso.*
ROSA LIKSOM, *Dark Paradise.*
OSMAN LINS, *Avalovara.*
  The Queen of the Prisons of Greece.
ALF MAC LOCHLAINN,
  The Corpus in the Library.
  Out of Focus.
RON LOEWINSOHN, *Magnetic Field(s).*
MINA LOY, *Stories and Essays of Mina Loy.*
BRIAN LYNCH, *The Winner of Sorrow.*
D. KEITH MANO, *Take Five.*
MICHELINE AHARONIAN MARCOM,
  The Mirror in the Well.
BEN MARCUS,
  The Age of Wire and String.
WALLACE MARKFIELD,
  Teitlebaum's Window.
  To an Early Grave.
DAVID MARKSON, *Reader's Block.*
  Springer's Progress.
  Wittgenstein's Mistress.
CAROLE MASO, *AVA.*
LADISLAV MATEJKA AND KRYSTYNA
  POMORSKA, EDS.,
  Readings in Russian Poetics:
  Formalist and Structuralist Views.
HARRY MATHEWS,
  The Case of the Persevering Maltese:
  Collected Essays.
  Cigarettes.
  The Conversions.
  The Human Country: New and
  Collected Stories.
  The Journalist.

FOR A FULL LIST OF PUBLICATIONS, VISIT:
www.dalkeyarchive.com

SELECTED DALKEY ARCHIVE PAPERBACKS

FOR A FULL LIST OF PUBLICATIONS, VISIT:
www.dalkeyarchive.com

SELECTED DALKEY ARCHIVE PAPERBACKS

FOR A FULL LIST OF PUBLICATIONS, VISIT:
www.dalkeyarchive.com